The
ONLY LIGHT
IN
LONDON

BOOKS BY LILY GRAHAM

Lily Graham
The
ONLY LIGHT
IN
LONDON

Bookouture

Published by Bookouture in 2024

An imprint of Storyfire Ltd.
Carmelite House
50 Victoria Embankment
London EC4Y 0DZ

www.bookouture.com

ISBN: 978-1-83790-649-9
eBook ISBN: 978-1-83790-648-2

For Frankie

PROLOGUE

LONDON, OCTOBER 1940

The bombs were making it impossible to read.

Finley's hands shook as she clutched her magazine. She was trying to focus on an article about how you could make carrots taste like meat if you put your mind to it, but she couldn't be fooled. And not just about the versatility of carrots.

Her body was like a radio dial tuned in to the hell being unleashed on the streets of London above. The crowded Underground station in Notting Hill Gate, where she was huddled along with her neighbours, was full of the soupy, anxious chatter of people taking refuge.

Finley couldn't seem to stop her body from shivering.

All the pamphlets and demonstrations of what to do during an air raid had been replaced inside her mind with the grisly scenes from what had happened the week before at the deep Tube station, Balham. A bomb had fallen on the road above the northern end of the platform tunnel, causing it to partially collapse and fill with earth and water. Over sixty people had died.

The destruction had been incomprehensible and it didn't even suffer a direct hit, which was everyone's worst fear. It had been a horrible shock. Until then the Underground had felt like the only safe place to Finley. She had taken down books to read, spent the evenings catching up with her friends and neighbours, and, despite the smell, the noise, and the lack of sanitation, she never minded too much because of what being down here meant.

That felt like an illusion now.

She blew out her cheeks and tried to calm down. She was letting herself down. Unable to keep her side up, as she had been doing for so long. But the thing is: sometimes you just can't keep calm or carry on; sometimes you just fall quickly apart.

From the painful sound of someone trying hard to stifle their sobs nearby, clearly she wasn't the only one feeling the strain tonight.

Finley turned and saw an old man sitting on a battered suitcase with his grey head in his hands. His shoulders were heaving while he cried silent sobs that he was trying desperately to stifle with white-knuckled fists.

Her heart lurched. She knew him. It was Mr Burns, her postman. He looked like he'd aged overnight; the papery skin on his face was crumpled in sorrow.

Finley chewed on her lip for a moment in indecision, then she thought in her mother's sternest voice, *right, that's quite enough of this, Prudence Finley*, which did the trick. She made her way over on unsteady legs to see what she could do to help him. She might not be able to change much for herself at the moment, but maybe she could offer him a sympathetic ear at the very least.

He looked up when she touched his shoulder, and the desolate look on his face pierced her soul. It was like looking at a stranger, instead of someone she'd known half her life.

She swallowed. 'Mr Burns. I wish I had some whisky to offer you,' she whispered. She could do with one herself (possibly even a double). 'But you can use this,' she said, giving him a clean handkerchief.

His fingers trembled as he took it from her and began to mop his eyes. 'Th-thanks, Prudence,' he said softly.

Finley forgave him for using her first name, under the circumstances.

'Is there anything I can do?'

'Turn back time?' he asked, giving her a ghost of a smile, before his chin began to quiver.

It was heartbreaking to witness. Finley's throat turned dry. 'I wish I could,' she said in a small, cracked voice.

He'd been her postman since she was a child, and they had always had long conversations at her front door about everything: from their favourite Shakespeare plays to their mutual love for old-fashioned roses, as well as the state of her star-crossed career. She'd never known him to be anything less than cheery before. A bit like herself, really.

Well, *usually*.

Mr Burns was one of the few who still thought she had a chance of becoming a lead actress in the West End, when even her mother now changed the subject or increasingly mentioned the value of a secretarial course whenever Finley said she was off to another audition. But Mr Burns always maintained that she shouldn't give up hope. He knew all about fortitude in the face of life's hardships, because with a bum knee and a goal to get into the postal service he knew all about the importance of perseverance. His pep talks whenever he caught her before she was off for another audition always buoyed her up.

For some reason, seeing him like this, so raw and exposed, felt almost shocking, like seeing him naked.

She wished there was something more she could do. Somehow, she didn't think the article from *Woman's Own* on mock meats would provide much comfort for him, either...

She knew that misery loved company but Finley didn't

want to add to his fears with her own, so she kept her response to his suggestion that she turn back time light. It was the kindest thing she could do under the circumstances.

'You know, if I *could* turn back time,' she said, with a wry grin, exposing small, ever so slightly crooked white teeth, 'I'd pop over to Germany and hunt down Hitler the day he decided to sport that silly moustache. I don't have scientific proof,' she added, giving him a wink, 'but I figure it is likely the moment he became properly evil, so it would be safe to throttle him with my bare hands.'

Mr Burns emitted a surprised, rather damp chuckle. 'Quite safe, yes,' he snorted, before his face, which had momentarily brightened, resumed its veil of sadness. His chin shook again and he took a few steadying breaths. 'Oh lord, I'm sorry, love, I feel like I'm letting the side down, being such a defeatist,' he said. He seemed utterly mortified with himself.

Finley's heart lurched for him. 'Mr Burns, please don't worry, I've been feeling *exactly* the same. Ever since Balham, it's all got a bit too real,' she admitted.

He nodded. 'I know, I keep thinking about that too. I know the Nazis don't deserve our panic, but things just got the better of me tonight,' he admitted.

Finley agreed. 'I'll be honest, it was easier when it just felt like we were going through the motions. When we knew the air raids were just tests, like in June.'

Going to her local air raid precaution training sessions to learn about the kinds of bombs that were likely to be dropped, and experiencing the horrible simulations of the poisonous gases the enemy might use and identifying the different scents, had been scary. As had been carrying around a gas mask everywhere she went; but this was real.

Too real.

He nodded. 'It's William I'm worrying about. I'm terrified of losing him. He's out there battling the skies, again, after he almost died a few months ago – what if his luck runs out? And all the while his dad is down here hiding? It just doesn't feel right.'

His voice broke and Finley bit her top lip to stop it from wobbling in response. *The poor man.* His son, William, was all he had left in the world. William had been one of the brave souls who had fought in June, in the Battle of Britain, as it would later be called, preventing the Germans from occupying them as they had planned.

'Mr Burns, I don't think luck works that way, and I bet for William keeping you safe is what's worth fighting for. It probably gives him the courage to carry on. I know I'd feel like that if it were my father. I'd have him back in a shot if it meant I had to go and drop bombs on Germany.'

Mr Burns nodded. His eyes turned soft as he considered her. 'He was a good man, your dad.'

Finley had to look away for a second, feeling the sting of tears, despite the passage of time. They had lost him when she was just seven years old, in the last war. It had been years, but sometimes it felt like it was only yesterday that she was being woken up to be told that he was gone. It was like a part of her had split in two that morning. The girl who'd gone to bed with both parents alive and the girl who woke up afterwards. And now she was terrified of history repeating itself.

Her mother had lost the man she had loved in the last war and now... well, she herself was in danger of meeting the same fate.

She had fallen for a man who had turned her whole world upside down since the first day she had laid eyes on him.

Sebastien Raphael was a beautiful Jewish refugee with the saddest eyes she'd ever seen, who had made her rethink everything she ever thought she knew about love or marriage or what she wanted out of life. She'd thought that she would likely be a spinster for ever, albeit hopefully with a wonderful career, but now all she wanted was him. He was just as much her dream now, as acting had been – but having the chance to have a life with him felt just as impossible now with the war on. He'd broken her heart the day he told her he'd signed up to fight.

He'd told her shortly after her little brother had broken the news that he had volunteered, and it had felt as if they'd both ripped her heart in two, straight out of her chest, and taken the pieces with them.

She knew it wasn't easy being the one who went off to fight, but sometimes she thought it was harder being the one left behind. The helplessness of it could eat you alive if you let it. Some days she lost the battle. Others, she could paint on a smile and pretend that everything was okay. Today wasn't one of them.

She gasped when a loud blast above made the walls reverberate so much that a cloud of dust began to fall from the ceiling.

They say you don't hear the bomb that came for you, thought Finley. Hearing the near-constant blasts was a good thing then, she reminded herself. But it was pointless trying to convince her shaking limbs of this.

'I think we're safe here,' said Mr Burns, seeing her pale face. It made her reddish-brown curls stand out all the more. It was his turn to reassure her now. 'They're not landing close,' he whispered, turning an ear to listen, then giving her hand a squeeze. Even though it was likely impossible for him to really know that, Finley felt comforted by him and his assurances. It was funny how that worked down here. How fast things turned. She squeezed his hand back.

'Thank you, for coming to save me from myself,' he whispered. 'I didn't realise how much I needed someone to distract me from my bleak thoughts.' He took a shuddery breath and looked around. 'We all do, I suppose.'

She nodded. She was just the same; like many of her neighbours. They were like small boats battling the fear in waves. It could wash over you or make you drown. A woman near the stairs was going under. They could all hear her wailing.

'Pull yourself together,' someone shouted at her.

'The Jerries don't deserve it,' said an older voice she recognised – clear as a bell, coming from the other side of the platform. 'If we go, we shouldn't give them the satisfaction!'

Finley turned, and saw that it was her friend, Archie Greeves. He was a librarian in his late sixties, with white hair and twinkly blue eyes above a rather crooked nose that made him all the more endearing somehow.

Behind him were Sunella Singh and Anita Hardglass. The members of the small amateur dramatics group she had formed, a year before, in a last bid to help launch her career. But in the end the group had done so much more than that. They'd been a life raft in a world drowning under so much conflict.

She hadn't seen them until now!

She felt a stab of pride when she considered how shy Archie used to be. How his voice used to shake with nerves whenever he tried to perform; *but just look at him now*, she thought.

Seeing him be so brave, something in her took courage and thought, *maybe we can help*. The way the group had helped her by making her feel less alone.

She gave him a signal, and he looked confused and mouthed 'what?' at her, so she stood up, gathered her courage around her like an old worn cloak, and straightened her spine.

She closed her eyes for a beat and thought of *their* poem. The one Sebastien had shared with them all, not long after he'd joined the amateur dramatics group, mostly by accident, one night when he was looking for shelter and stumbled across them. Lonely and friendless, in the weeks that followed, he had opened up and had shared with them a poem that helped him after he fled the Nazis and made a new life in a strange country.

After that they couldn't help but become so much more than just a group with a love of Shakespeare in common; they became friends. In the months after war was declared, the poem became almost sacred to them; a call to courage for everything they now faced.

They could do all do with that now.

Finley took a deep breath, her face sombre in the low station light, as she began to speak.

A hush fell as people turned in surprise and listened.

> *Out of the night that covers me,*
> *black as the pit from pole to pole,*
> *I thank whatever gods may be for my unconquer-*
> > *able soul.*

There was a gasp. People were staring. Some were muttering. Her throat turned dry. Part of her thought, was this a mistake? But *no*, they all needed something else to think about. Something beside the fear.

Finley's cream blouse with the Peter Pan collar felt as if it were choking her and her palms were sweating; she rubbed them against her long, blue tweed skirt as she shook in her high-heeled brown brogues. Then she gave Archie the signal again, hoping he'd understand. The people near her turned to look in the direction she was indicating. A low hubbub of voices erupted around them. Someone clapped and then stopped. A woman in a headscarf with bright-red lipstick was staring at her open-mouthed. There was a whispering hum of expectancy as more and more people looked in her direction. Finley swallowed, waiting for Archie to take the reins now.

At last he nodded, and straightened. He looked nervous. His old, dear face flickered with emotion. Then his melodic voice rose over them, as he recited the next verse.

He was perfect. So perfect. Finley felt tears smart behind her warm brown eyes.

In the fell clutch of circumstance
I have not winced nor cried aloud.
Under the bludgeonings of chance my head is
      bloody, but unbowed.

Next came Sunella Singh's clear, girlish voice as she continued the poem. She was beautiful in a red sari, her dark eyes magnetic.

Finley closed her eyes, and a tear slid down her cheek.

Anita followed, her deep voice loud and carrying, lending the gravitas that Henley's words inspired.

The air around them had changed, as if collectively the station had begun to release a breath they'd all been holding.

Never had Finley felt each word of the poem down to her very bones, until now.

Even though Sebastien was out there fighting, for a moment it felt as if they were all together again.

Someone whispered, 'That's beautiful.' It felt like the smallest curl of hope was beginning to spread. Like signs of green after a long winter.

Around her she could hear some of the others whispering.

'Did they plan this?'

'Are they from the West End?'

'Is it a play of some kind? I heard they were going to start advertising for amateur dramatic society groups, like this, to entertain us?'

She hadn't planned this, it wasn't anything they did for anyone but them, and they certainly weren't from the West End. A factor that, at one time, Finley would have given anything to change. But that was before. Before she had met

Sebastien. Before she had changed, thanks to them. Thanks to *him*.

Now, from opposite ends of the platform, they delivered the last verse together, their voices swelling the platform. Drowning out anything else, including their shared panic of what might lie in wait.

> *It matters not how strait the gate,*
> *how charged with punishments the scroll,*
> *I am the master of my fate,*
> *I am the captain of my soul.*

A cheer rang out across the platform. The wailing had stopped, replaced now with raised chins and straightened spines. Finley turned to look at her friends and neighbours, and felt her limbs stop shaking at long last.

They might not be able to choose how this would end. Whether they would leave this station dead or alive. What was in their hands though was the choice they could make now on how they would face this night.

Together.

Bloody, perhaps, but unbowed.

EIGHT MONTHS BEFORE

1

LONDON, MARCH 1939

'The thing is, Prudence, darling, you're just *not* right for the part.'

Finley, who was twenty-eight, and never used her first name if she could help it, had been working her way up to the finale in Portia's 'pound of flesh' speech from *The Merchant of Venice*, only to deflate like a balloon with a slow puncture.

She shaded her amber-coloured eyes with a manicured hand, her fingernails painted in her luckiest red shade, as she peered into the stands, where the director, Nigel Fitzpatrick, was slumped over in the third row, looking for all the world as if someone's dog had died.

'I could come in with a bit more gumption,' suggested Finley, who was one of life's natural optimists. 'I was going for more of a dramatic build-up, but I can give it a bit more welly, really open up?' she offered, brightly, her brown curls turning auburn in the overhead lights.

Nigel broke into a cough that sounded suspiciously like he was covering up a laugh. 'Honestly, Prudence, it does not lack, erm, *welly*.'

Finley narrowed her eyes and he had the grace to look a little shamefaced.

This only made things worse.

Finley's stomach plummeted as she considered the terrible possibility that she was awful at the only thing she had ever really wanted out of life. Being the lead actress in a play in the West End was her dream. From the first time she had been taken to the theatre by her father at the age of six, and had seen the way everyone on that stage all seemed to be dreaming aloud together, something in her had come alive and thought, *maybe I could do this.* Followed very quickly by the goal that some day she would be just like the beautiful lead actress on stage who was enchanting them.

Unfortunately, so far *that* hadn't quite gone to plan...

She'd worked for years, with some success in smaller roles, but nothing in the major leagues. But there was still time, she was sure. One day, a top director would look past her round face, short frame and reddish-brown hair and give her the chance to star...

Surely.

But what if something else was letting her down?

What if she just wasn't good enough?

What if her mother was right and it really was time to Be Sensible About Things and Get a Proper Job? Give up the helter-skelter life of a jobbing actress who did everything from pantomimes to community theatre and bit parts in the big plays?

There is a first time for anything, thought Finley, who wasn't known for being sensible, or listening to her mother for that matter.

She took a deep, courageous breath and said, 'If I am a ham, Nigel, you can tell me.'

Nigel stared at her in confusion. 'A ham?' he repeated, rubbing rather bloodshot eyes.

'A ham actor – you know? Overdoing things. It seemed to be what you were suggesting earlier when you said I was giving it enough welly,' she said, feeling uncharacteristically nervous. She fiddled with the pearl earrings her mother had bought her on her sixteenth birthday. A lucky charm.

'Oh!' he said, then started to laugh.

Finley frowned. This *was* serious.

He shook his head when he saw the look on her face. 'I didn't mean *that*. It was the right welly, darling,' he said rummaging in his discarded blazer for his cigarettes. He lit one, took a drag, then sighed. 'To be honest, you're the best I've seen in a week. A natural, sadly.'

He did look rather sad about that. 'Really?' she said, feeling buoyed for a moment, only to sink low once more as the word 'sadly' hung in the air amid the smoke.

'Is it the height difference between the lead and me? Because Bill said he'd stoop a little, and I can wear higher heels...' Surely, if she was the best an experienced casting director like him had seen, something could be done!

Nigel sighed. 'Even if somehow that could work—'

'Oh, it will! Why don't we try it out?' She beamed, her dark eyes shining winningly. 'If you stand on this chair and stoop a little, I'll go on my tiptoes, and then you'll see what I mean.'

Finley's smile was rather transformative. Bright-red lipstick, not perfectly straight teeth but the sort of *joie de vivre* that could not be faked. It lit up the room, and made one think she was prettier than she was, particularly when she had a mind to be charming, as she was then.

For a moment, Nigel Fitzpatrick felt genuine regret, but unfortunately for Finley the stress of being up to his eyeballs in debt, combined with an expensive West End Shakespeare production and producers who were starting to demand that he actually produce something, meant that he could not afford to take a risk and hire someone who might actually be able to do the part justice. He needed the sort of face that would sell tickets, not loads of baked goods at a local fete.

'Look,' admitted Nigel. 'It's not just the height.'

Ah. Here it comes, thought Finley with a sigh.

When it did, it was worse than usual, though. Nigel ran a hand through his sandy blond hair, looking awkward. 'Look Prudence, you've got to realise you aren't quite leading lady material. It can't be a *surprise* at this point.'

Finley flinched, the way he made it out, she would be better placed to audition to be a troll under a bridge. 'You're not exactly an oil painting yourself, Nige,' she pointed out, equally helpfully.

'I am not trying out for a lead part in a West End play!'

He had her there.

Finley stared at him and he continued, softening. 'I don't mean to imply you are unattractive, honestly, darling, under the right lighting and that sort of thing you are quite appealing, particularly when you smile.'

Finley scoffed, 'Careful there, Nigel, my legs might go weak if you lay on any more charm.'

He pursed his lips, then took a drag of his cigarette, explaining on his exhale. 'What I mean is, Prudence, you look like the girl next door, pleasant, pretty almost, but just not quite "it", you know?'

'Even Ginger Rogers was somebody's girl next door,' she pointed out. Ordinarily, she would have given in by now, but he had said she was the best he'd seen, and *a natural*. She tried to ignore the pretty *almost* part.

'Yes, well she doesn't look it.' Then he frowned and his eyes lit up with an idea. 'What if you lost a little weight? That might help – I mean not for the lead, obviously... but a more substantial support role, perhaps?'

'I weigh nine stone!'

She didn't quite, actually, but damn him to *hell*.

'Do you really?' he said, eyes widening as he looked her up and down, and seeming to like what he saw, from the neck down at least. 'Oh yes, I see. How unfortunate – so your face is just naturally that round?'

'Yes,' said Finley with all the grace of a sad clown whose lapel flower has started raining in their eyes.

'Like I said, er, Prudence. It's just that nowadays, with the influence of Hollywood, the standards are just a bit higher, people want glamour, perfection. Tall, striking, imposing even. They don't want to see someone so, well, *ordinary* as their leading lady. The men want a bit of fantasy, the women, some aspiration, you know?'

Oh, Finley knew. Some of the other casting directors had suggested quite ludicrous things over the years – one had even suggested she pluck the hair on her forehead to create a widow's peak. Being called ordinary smarted, but she knew it *shouldn't*. The world was full of ordinary people, so why not show it? She didn't really relate to bombshells and she suspected many women didn't either...

On cue, Nigel offered his own 'helpful' suggestion. 'You know, Vita Norfolk had her back teeth removed and it did wonders for her, she went from chorus girl to supporting star overnight. You might want to consider that, eh, old sport?'

She blinked. She had endured him calling her Prudence with gritted teeth but this took the blooming cake. *Old sport?* Who in the blazes did he think he was? F. Scott Fitzgerald's *Gatsby?*

Her round face coloured like a setting sun. She narrowed her eyes. 'Is that what they did to you?'

'What, pulled out my back teeth?' he asked, touching his jawline in surprise. 'No, why do you ask?'

'Well, I thought that might explain what happened to your brain – perhaps they pulled too far back and took it out?'

· · ·

The thing is, thought Finley, as she stomped out of the Regent with a firm black mark against her name, Nigel Fitzpatrick's shouts that she 'would never make it out of pantos with an attitude like that!' ringing in her ears as she made her way down Shaftesbury Avenue, character acting was surely the ticket? You didn't need to be attractive for that. She could even put on weight, stop plucking her eyebrows and maybe get a wart on the end of her nose – there was always a part for a witch.

This cheered her up somewhat, until she passed a newsstand and frowned. She'd tried really hard not to worry about recent events but, with Hitler going back on his word about the Munich Agreement, the whispers about war had started again.

In September, Czechoslovakia had reluctantly agreed to cede the parts of the Sudetenland where three million people of German origin were living to Germany, in the hopes that he wouldn't occupy them, but now he'd done it anyway.

Her stomach did a horrible flip. She just didn't know what she would do if they had another war. It had taken years to put her family back together again after the last one when they lost her father.

At age seven, Finley had had to face the fact that she would never again see her wonderful father who had lit up her whole world. Worse, she had to deal with a pregnant mother, who had sunk into a depression for months. They'd got through it all and come out stronger on the other side. But it had been a hard battle and she really didn't know if she could face something like that again.

Then there was the fact that her 21-year-old brother Christopher had said that he would volunteer if war broke out. It had shocked Finley to her core. The last war had robbed Christopher of ever meeting his father – their mother was pregnant with him when he died. So he knew better than anyone the cost of war.

She hadn't spoken to him for a week after he told her that,

and she usually found it impossible to be cross at her blue-eyed, mischievous brother for longer than five minutes. That was how deeply the idea of him risking his life had upset her. The thought of him being taken from them too turned her blood cold. When she'd told her mother what he'd said, Isabelle had only half-jokingly said she would lock him in his room to keep him safe and Finley had replied, 'If it comes to that, I'll install the bolt myself.'

Last year, when Chamberlain was certain he'd brokered a peace deal and had proclaimed, 'Peace for our Time', she, along with others who had lost so much in the Great War, had felt grateful to the allied leaders and their efforts to appease Hitler in order to prevent war. Even though she had felt bad for the Czechoslovakians forced into a bit of a cowardly plan by their allies, she, like many others, had also thought that it was likely a dirty, but necessary business to appease Hitler and prevent further conflict.

And now it had all been for nothing?

She tore her gaze away from the papers, determined not to dwell on it.

No one wanted another war.

2

That afternoon, backstage at the smallest theatre in the West End, the Glory (where the irony was not lost on anyone), Muriel, an attractive woman in her early forties, with honey-blond hair, turned the dial of the radio in the middle of the news broadcast, where the focus remained on Hitler's violation of the Munich Agreement.

Muriel had lost her sweetheart in the last war, and her fingers shook as she looked for a different station.

Her deep-blue eyes looked haunted for a moment. 'That's better,' she said, as cheering jazz music swelled the room, and she began to sway along to Louis Armstrong, who was singing, *I'm in the mood for love.*

The costume department was a small, cosy room, crammed full of dressmaker's dummies, yards of fabric that spilled over plump velvet chairs and wall-to-ceiling shelves stacked with buttons and lace and sparkly trimmings that would cause a magpie's heart to swell.

Finley, who was tucked into a green velvet Queen Anne chair in the corner, near the tiny bar heater, nodded in agreement as she worked on the blush-pink Regency dress she was hemming for a small production of Jane Austen's *Sense and Sensibility* (for which she had been turned down). She worked part-time as a costume assistant when she was between theatre roles.

'I'm guessing you didn't get the part,' said Muriel with a kind smile, putting down the bolero she was beading onto a small end table.

Finley frowned, looking up and biting a piece of thread with her teeth, careful not to get red lipstick on it. 'Why do you say that?'

'Well, as you haven't said more than "hello" since you got here, I took a gamble. It's either that or the news getting you down.' Muriel bit her lip, then brightened. 'Usually you can talk for England. I was sort of hoping for that today,' she admitted.

No one wanted to think of the state of the world at present. Even here in the light of the make-believe confines of the theatre, the shadows of the world outside were creeping in, despite Louis Armstrong's warm voice.

Finley sighed. 'Sorry. It's a bit of both really, the news, and yes... my career, or lack of one at the moment.'

The parts had been drying up and sometimes she worried she really would have to be *sensible* at some point.

Muriel's eyes were full of sympathy. 'Cup of tea?'

Finley smiled at her, gratefully. 'Love one.'

When Muriel returned with a tray topped with a red and gold teapot and matching porcelain cups, and made her a cup, she looked thoughtfully at Finley who had just taken her first sip and said, 'What about trying Sorry Johnny?'

Finley spluttered tea down the front of her pale-blue blouse with its tiny seed buttons, and then half-laughed as she frowned at Muriel while she mopped it up with the tea towel. 'Oh Muriel, you *promised* you'd stop calling him that.'

Muriel gave her big eyes, then bit her lip to suppress a giggle as she sank into the velvet chair opposite Finley, next to a bolt of green chiffon. 'I know, darling, but the poor lamb, I can't help but feel sorry for him. I mean, he's divine to look at too...' She grinned, mischievously.

Finley rolled her eyes, but she couldn't help a small laugh.

'Sorry Johnny' was what Muriel called her ex (whose name was actually Simon Alexander) because Finley had had to write him a 'Dear John letter' when she had turned down his marriage proposal last year.

Finley had really liked Simon, maybe even loved him a little, or she could have, in time, but she could just see how their life would have been if she'd said yes. Which was part of the problem. It would have been a good life, but it wouldn't have been the one she wanted. Mainly because he thought she should give up her career.

Simon had seemed to think that once they got married she would stop being an actress. It had been a frequent fight. Despite the fact that he managed a theatre pub, he had strong opinions about how he wanted his home life to be: *conventional*. A wife at home in a house with a garden, two or three children and perhaps a cat. She'd been up for all of it, apart from the wife at home bit and giving up on her career for no real reason aside from his masculine pride. Also the cat, she being more of a dog person.

But the rest, yes. Simon hadn't wanted to bend quite as much as Finley, though; she'd even offered to bend on the cat part.

She looked at Muriel and said hotly, 'I didn't think you would turn into my mother – I fail one audition, so now I should give up on acting and settle down with Simon?'

Muriel shook her head and laughed. 'Of course not, darling, you can't go into a marriage hoping to change the other, divorce number two convinced me of *that*. I have always supported your choice, even if I did think it was a pity we wouldn't be seeing him around anymore.' She winked, 'No. I just meant, well, he manages that pub on Shaftesbury Avenue that puts on amateur productions, All the World's a Stage, yes?'

It took its name from Shakespeare, naturally.

'Yes?'

'Well, I've heard that George Vaughn cast his new lead from a small production he saw there.'

Finley gasped in shock. 'He didn't!'

Muriel's red-manicured fingers toyed with her gold necklace, as she stared at Finley meaningfully. 'He most certainly did.'

George Vaughn was one of the best playwrights in the business and everyone had been talking about the leading lady in his new smash hit play; she was supposed to be sensational.

'Apparently, Vaughn said she was perfect for the role and went over the director's head and, well, considering how well that play is doing, he was totally right, too.'

Finley stared at Muriel, who nodded as if she could read her mind. 'I *know*. Apparently, it's become a big hot spot for talent scouts now. Everyone's trying to get noticed there.'

Muriel always knew what was happening in the business.

Finley couldn't believe it. That had happened in Simon's pub?

'What if you put in a word with Sorry Johnny and tried to get in on one of those amateur productions he always supports? I'm sure he could point you to the right company,' suggested Muriel.

Finley looked doubtful. 'I don't know.'

Muriel nodded. 'He still cares for you – if you could somehow get a production going, he'd definitely let you perform there, I'm sure,' she suggested.

Finley blinked. 'My own production?'

Muriel frowned. 'Sorry, that came out wrong, I meant if you could get going in a production there... it could open some doors?'

Muriel might not have meant it that way, but she'd definitely planted a seed... one that grew as the afternoon turned to evening. By the time Finley was on her second Tube home to Notting Hill, the idea had firmly taken root.

What if she started her own amateur dramatics society? Where she could call the shots? Like cast *herself* in the lead?

Perhaps Simon *would* allow her to use his venue to stage a production? There was even the chance that he might come round, and see that she didn't need to give up her dream for them to work as a couple...

But even if he didn't, if All the World's a Stage had become a hot spot, perhaps someone like George Vaughn would see beyond her round face, small stature and ordinariness!

At dinner, though, she was so lost in her own dream world of seeing herself as a leading lady of the West End and of Nigel Fitzpatrick begging for her forgiveness and asking for her to star in his next play, she didn't hear what her mother was saying.

'Sorry?' she said, putting down her fork with its bit of dry pork chop back onto her plate.

Her mother's grey eyes had turned steely like she was weathering some internal storm. Finley felt a stab of empathy for her; she knew practical, sensible, Isabelle struggled with her daughter sometimes and found it difficult to relate to Finley's rose-tinted view that everything would work out for the best.

Isabelle had turned to her favourite topic. Sorting out Finley's life.

'I was just saying that since this audition didn't go to plan, the one you assured me was "the one", and since you haven't been cast in anything for a while, maybe it's time you looked for a steadier job...?'

Finley sighed. Here we go, she thought.

'...rent has gone up and my shop, you know, doesn't bring in a fortune.'

Contrary to her pleas of poverty, her mother owned a well-beloved local haberdashery shop that Finley knew for a fact did more than well enough for their needs. She forgot that her daughter helped her with the books. Finley might have her head in the clouds most of the time but she was also rather good at mathematics.

Since her father had died, her mother was the main bread-winner of the family. Her husband's war pension didn't cover everything; and with Christopher, her pride and joy, reading for a degree in law at Oxford, some extra money was always welcome.

Finley bit her lip. It wasn't that she didn't want to lessen her mother's load. Lord knew she tried – she had two part-time jobs at the moment, and she was going for every audition around – but for Isabelle there was always a reason as to why it wasn't quite good enough...

On cue, her mother said, 'I'm sorry, darling, but you need to pull your weight a bit more. You're too old to be carrying on like this. A part-time costume assistant, and three evenings a week as a coat-check girl at *that* jazz club.'

Isabelle always referred to it as *that* jazz club. Even though it was actually a very respectable place, which Finley happened to love.

'These are not real jobs. I mean how many failed auditions will it be, Finley, before you decide to just be sensible? You're nearly thirty,' she said, in exasperation, and gave Finley a pointed look. 'It's not like you're getting any more marriage proposals to squander.'

Finley sighed. 'I'm twenty-eight, I haven't been put out to pasture quite yet.'

Her mother raised a brow, as if to disagree.

'And I did not squander Simon's proposal,' added Finley hotly. 'I very carefully turned him down.' It had been one of the hardest things she had done.

Isabelle tutted. 'You broke that poor boy's heart.'

Finley frowned. 'Well, he broke mine too. What about my heart, my dreams, Mummy? Why is it always okay for women to give up their wants, their desires, but we turn a blind eye when a man doesn't even bend a little to support the woman they *say* they love?'

To her shock, her mother nodded. 'It's not right. I think he was a fool too.'

Finley blinked. 'Oh?'

Her mother's lips quirked into a mischievous grin and for just a moment it was possible to see a little of Finley's effervescence in the older woman. 'He should have kept quiet about wanting you to quit acting and let it happen naturally – after a few children I doubt you would have had the energy to want to frolic on stage,' she said, but there was a lightness to her tone that meant that she was only teasing.

'Oh, I see,' said Finley with a snort. 'Silly Simon. Should have listened to Mummy.'

'With age comes great wisdom...'

Finley rolled her eyes.

Her mother's lips settled back into seriousness but her eyes had softened. 'I just want you to think about the future, darling, that's all. I didn't, and then look what happened after your father died... suddenly, I had to become mother and father to two children. Of course, I'd love it for your sake if your career took off. I support you, even if it probably feels sometimes like I don't. I just worry, and I want to know you're being sensible about things.'

Finley felt a pang for of love for her, mixed in with a fair amount of sheer exasperation. They probably both felt the same way about the other. Her mother had been around enough times when reality had come crashing down on Finley's head. She had warned Finley early on that Simon didn't seem the type who would like it if his wife worked, particularly in the arts, but Finley had convinced herself that her mother was wrong and Simon would come round. She knew Isabelle tried her best to be the voice of reason, but there were also times that her reasoning wasn't actually helpful, as it felt more like settling for something than trying for what she really wanted just for the sake of security.

For instance, even when Finley had steady acting work Isabelle worried about what would happen when it ran out, and the fact that she had turned Simon down was a constant thorn in her mother's side, mostly because financially it would have made more sense to have gone through with the marriage. Finley just couldn't live that way, even if that made things harder in the end. Her father's death had taught her how short life was and she didn't ever want to squander it by only half-living if she could help it. She didn't want to be someone who lived with regrets and she knew she would regret giving up on herself.

Finley knew exactly what was coming next, and she hastened to put her mother off.

'*Mother*, I'm not going to do a secretarial course, not now, not ever,' she warned, her brown eyes looking for a moment every bit as steely as her mother's.

'Now Prudence,' said her mother, who was just about to get to the part in her timeworn lecture about practicality and the real world. This was generally when she began calling her daughter by her birth name, in the hope that she would miraculously live up to it.

Finley headed her off. 'I'll speak to Muriel about going full-time. She's already said she could use me.'

Her mother looked shocked, almost as if she didn't quite believe her ears. 'Really?'

Finley nodded. 'I don't know how much more money that will bring in, maybe not enough, but—'

'That's all right, the shop covers us pretty well,' said her mother, in defiance of her earlier comments, with a big smile.

'The main thing is that it will be steady, and that is something to rely on,' she finished, approvingly.

Something to rely on was another one of Isabelle's beloved lectures. 'I'm glad to see you being more sensible about things, at last, Finley. Perhaps we could even get a lodger,' she said, warming to her theme.

Getting a lodger was the height of sensibleness in Isabelle's worldview, seeing as they lived in a three-bedroom house and one of those rooms was now empty when it could pay its way. They could always make up a bed in the dining room for Christopher when he came to visit in the holidays from university.

Finley smiled. It was always a good sign when Isabelle had moved on to the idea of getting a lodger. It meant she herself was out of the firing line.

Until she said, 'You might want to rethink *that* jazz club though.'

Finley sighed.

It was after midnight, her head in curlers and covered by a silk scarf, fortified with a glass of sherry, that Finley fed a fresh sheet of paper into her father's old Remington typewriter and stared at the blank page with determination.

The old wireless in her bedroom was softly playing swing music and she tapped her slippered foot along to the beat.

Then she touched the photograph on her dressing table of her father swinging Finley in his arms, his handsome face full of laughter, and took courage. His motto had always been, 'Do nothing small, least of all life!'

She thought about that at least once a day. Usually whenever she was doubting if she would ever get ahead in her career...

Of course, she would need Simon to agree to let her put on

an amateur dramatics production at his theatre pub, but she could beg him if she had to.

She grinned, feeling better than she had all day now that she had a plan.

Then as her mother slept on unawares in the room at the end of the corridor, perhaps dreaming of her extra lodger and a daughter who actually lived up to her birth name at last, Finley began to type up the advertisement that she was going to put in the local paper the very next day.

She might have agreed to go full-time as a costume assistant, but that didn't mean she was giving up on her dream. Playing small was *not* part of the plan.

Finley would worry about breaking the news to Isabelle tomorrow.

It seemed being sensible was not on today's list of things to do, after all.

JOIN THE FINLEY PLAYERS!

This is your chance to be a part of a brand new amateur dramatic society, headed up by a professional actress. This is a group that is Going Places. Think – Bright Lights! Experience is preferable, but enthusiasm and a love for the stage counts too. Let's create amazing productions together that will get everyone talking! Auditions will be held by director Prudence Finley at 7 p.m. on 20 March at the Thrifty Thimble. We will be reading from Romeo and Juliet, *please prepare a short piece to perform.*

3

LONDON, MARCH 1939

The Underground train was heaving with people on their way to work.

Sebastien Raphael held on to the metal bar above his head and swayed not from the motion, but from fatigue.

There were deep purple shadows beneath his vivid blue eyes and his frame was so thin that his jacket now looked two sizes too big for him.

It had been a long night at his second job, a mindless role at the canning factory forty minutes out of the city, and now he was heading to his day job, where, instead of getting to write as he had done back home in Berlin, he set the type for several newspapers at a printing press.

Still, he was lucky. He was here. A Jewish refugee, and a British citizen thanks to his British father, who had died shortly after he was born. It had allowed him to escape with just the clothes on his back when he fled Nazi Germany in August, on a night that sweltered with heat and fear and still left a bitter taste of regret in his mouth today.

As the train sped along he was pulled back to that awful warm night, five months before.

. . .

It was past eleven and Berlin was so humid that the fan just circulated the warm air around the shabby office downtown that they'd moved to in the past year. Sebastien undid another button of his navy shirt, then tapped his pen against his lip, which was dotted with sweat, as he re-read his latest searing political story, which exposed the truth – that the Nazi government and Hitler weren't as peace-loving as they pretended to be. That war was actually their end goal.

It was his most daring article yet. In the current climate, being critical of the Nazi Party was an enormous risk, and they had to go about it surreptitiously or risk having their newspaper shut down or, worse, face jail time.

In the last edition, which appeared at first glance to be a praise piece on a Nazi minister, they had sneaked in a damning account of the minister's involvement in a financial scandal.

He rubbed his tired dark-blue eyes, then spotted a typographical error and was just about to address it when he heard the sound of hastening footsteps, followed by the slam of the metal door as it crashed against the wall. He stood up fast, fear flooding his senses at the thought of being discovered here.

Lotte, the editor, Samuel's wife and the paper's secretary, raced in, her heels beating a sharp tattoo against the parquet floor. Her long black hair was tied up in a silk scarf and she was uncharacteristically make-up-less. Despite the heat, she was wearing a green housecoat, under which he could see the slip of a cream nightdress. She must have raced here. His heart skipped a beat. He had known that some day this might happen.

'Sebastien! she shouted as she burst in. 'They've taken Samuel for questioning. Someone must have informed the authorities that you are working here illegally.'

Sebastien was Jewish. It was forbidden for him to work in journalism. It was why he worked at night, in secret, and why his articles appeared under a false name. He turned pale. He couldn't let his boss take the fall for him. Even though Samuel had suggested he begin working under false papers when the new ruling that Jews couldn't work for the press came into force, Sebastien couldn't let him go to prison! He'd tell them it was his fault, his idea...

'Where is he? I'll go – I will explain. I'll tell them he didn't know!'

'Don't be a fool,' she snapped, harsher than she usually was. Tears shimmered in her eyes. 'They'll put you both in prison then – or worse! Besides it will be easy enough to prove he knew, as you'd worked here for years before they changed the rules.'

The words 'or worse' ricocheted in his mind, leaving behind black holes that rippled through him, full of dark possibility.

Lotte was firm. 'He said to tell you to get out of Berlin. You must go tonight, now!'

Sebastien hesitated. 'B-but I can't just let Samuel take the blame, Lotte, what will happen to him – you have children!'

Her jaw flexed and she looked fierce and determined. She wiped away an angry tear. 'He won't. I'll make sure of that – I will talk to his sister Elfriede tonight. Beg her if I have to. They have their differences, but she does love her brother.'

Samuel's sister was married to a senior member of the Nazi Party, which had caused a big rift between them, but Sebastien had long suspected it was why the paper hadn't as yet been closed down. There was the chance that she might be able to use her connections to keep her brother safe.

The same could not be said for Sebastien.

Lotte seemed to be reading his mind because she said, 'You could get shot for what you've written about that minister. I knew that was a mistake! The two of you – always having to push, push, push. And now they suspect the truth – that Samuel kept you on even though you are Jewish, under false papers. But

they can't prove it if they can't find you! You'll be helping
Samuel by leaving.'

Sebastien blinked, knowing she had a point.

'If they can't find you they can't prove that you were writing
under an alias. I don't know if Elfriede will be able to help him
otherwise. Samuel is sticking to the story for now – that you
really are Harry Glass, and not Sebastien Raphael. But it will be
harder to do that if you're found here tonight. It's too easy to
prove that you're not. I wouldn't be surprised if you were on their
list.'

Sebastien closed his eyes in helpless horror for a moment.
Neither would he. He had been writing inflammatory pieces
long before it became illegal for him to do so. The soldiers
wouldn't have to go too far back in the paper's archives to find his
likeness.

Sebastien nodded, feeling torn, even though he knew she was
right – it didn't feel right at all. He couldn't stand the idea of
Samuel facing prison time. The thought of leaving the paper, of
leaving his life, though, made him feel ill. He felt a rush of hatred
towards the Nazis for all they had already taken from him; and
now they had won again. He'd tried so hard not to give in, not to
run away, to stay and fight. But what other choice did he
have now?

'I'll go.'

'Good.'

He'd taken the sleeper train to Rüdesheim, along the River
Rhine, near the border with France and Switzerland. His family
lived in this small village, near a vineyard. An idyllic place
where even now the shadows of the darkness that was gripping
Germany could be found.

He hoped he could convince them to follow him. To sneak
across the border with him.

'But Sebastien,' countered his stepfather, Gunther, a tall Jewish man with black hair and a kind smile, who'd been the only father Sebastien had ever known. 'It's not so simple for us. Even here they've begun patrolling the borders, there's a real danger of getting caught – we don't have the paperwork you have. Your birth father was British, so you have automatic citizenship. We need to do this right, and get our visas. Your mother lost her right to her British passport when your father died and she remarried... it's not as straight forward for us, son.'

Sebastien clasped his arm. 'Father, do we have the time to wait? Mrs Vintner in the flat above has that summer house in Switzerland, we could go and talk to her, I could drive us. Oskar Meyer, who forged our work papers, does visas now, too – I could get this all arranged fast.'

Oskar was a friend of his from university, a fine artist, who used his skills in ways he had never imagined he would a decade before, helping many of their friends to flee. He lived in nearby Cologne, and it wouldn't take that long to arrange.

'It's too risky, Sebastien,' snapped his mother, Marta. 'We can't ask that of Mrs Vintner, or Oskar!' Her face was a picture of worry. Her dark hair was in its customary chignon, and she rubbed at her ear nervously, touching a diamond and pearl earring, a relic from another time, when they used to live a very different kind of life in Berlin, before they moved to this tiny flat in Rüdesheim, where they had hoped the officials wouldn't be quite as rigorous as in the big city. They were on much-reduced salaries and had had to relinquish most of their assets to the Nazis, who demanded them in another of their ludicrous rules.

Even here in this small, lovely village, the hatred for Jews had begun to spread. The friends that they had made had begun to turn away; how long before they turned against them too? Soon enough Gunther might have to also face questioning, as he was also working on false papers. His profession had become illegal for Jews too.

'Mama, surely by now we should think of taking risks. They already treat us like criminals for a crime we did not commit,' said Sebastien. 'Only allowed to travel third class, not allowed to work in our chosen fields, practise medicine, or the law, or attend "their" cinemas and bars. We don't have to live this way. If we go to England, things will be different, and maybe one day when the Nazis are out we can come back.'

'Sebastien, it's never that simple. You don't remember as you were a baby, but I did that already. I lived in England with your birth father after the first war, his family disowned him for marrying a German Jew and wanted nothing to do with us' – she half-laughed – 'though it is ironic they hate me more for being German there. But still, the way we were treated there – oh it was horrible. Everywhere I went I was treated with contempt. It was so hard to make friends. When I came back here it was like I could breathe again. I just don't know if I could go back.'

'Mama, they're doing that here – and so much worse.'

She sighed. 'I know but we need to do it the right way. Oskar is taking a huge risk forging visas. Besides, we can't just go like that,' she said, snapping her fingers. 'Katrin hasn't finished the school year yet, we would need her transcripts... I think in a few months maybe we can look to come. Apply for the visas properly like your father says.'

Katrin was his half-sister. She was twelve years old, bright as a button, and full of life. He worried that the way things were going that light inside her might begin to dim, if she were forced to start believing the things the Nazis wanted people like her to believe about herself. That she wasn't good enough. He felt his anger flare again. Some days he felt he was drowning in it. He wished, not for the first time, that he would be able to fight them somehow.

His mother touched her neck in anxiety. 'It's not like in the city, where there's dozens of Party officers coming to check on these things. Gunther works in the back office of the pharmacy *here, no one sees him. Besides, it's a small village, we're on good terms with everyone, I wouldn't be surprised if most people around here know Gunther is Jewish and are turning a blind eye.'*

Sebastien raised a brow. 'Mama, until this evening I thought the same about all the people I work with – all my friends. It's a small paper, and we've known each other for ten years. But someone informed on us. It just takes one – one person who is perhaps terrified of what it will mean if they don't report him, or maybe someone who has swallowed all this garbage that Jews are the enemy... and then what? Think of Elke.'

His mother flinched. Elke was her best friend.

'She hasn't swallowed it. She's struggling too – it can't be easy to find yourself living with someone who has become so – so...' She searched for the right word.

'Radicalised?' offered Sebastien.

Marta nodded, looking sad. Elke was the main reason she and Gunther had moved to the countryside – because Elke had said it would be more welcoming. But now, Elke's husband was in the Nazi Party, and increasingly they were beginning to drift apart.

Sebastien shook his head. 'Mama, Elke is a ticking bomb and she knows about Gunther's papers. It's dangerous not to do anything. I was a fool not to see it myself. Now look, Samuel is in prison because of me—'

'Samuel knew the risk he was taking, it was his idea!'

His boss had become a close family friend over the years, and still took the time, at least once a year, to come visit them for a few days' holiday.

'It was both of ours,' denied Sebastien. 'But to save him, I need to go.'

His mother's lip wobbled, and she held a hand to her mouth to keep the emotion inside as she nodded.

'I don't want you to go!' cried Katrin, his little sister, bursting

into the room. Tears pouring down her cheeks. She'd clearly been listening at the door, a silent witness until then.

Sebastien felt a lump form in his throat, and he turned to hug her tight.

'I don't want to leave, Kat. I wish I didn't have to,' he whispered, feeling the sting of tears as he held on to his little sister, his little light in a world that had turned dark. The thought of not seeing her, of her not getting out too, was enough to make him gasp for air.

Marta could see the struggle on his face and she raced to put her arms round them both.

Gunther did the same. Marta's lips trembled. 'But you must, my darling, it won't be long before they come looking for you. Thank the lord you have your passport.'

He nodded, then clasped her hand while Katrin cried into his shoulder.

'We will be together again,' he said.

'You promise?' said Katrin.

'I promise,' said Sebastien. 'We will find a way.'

Sebastien had been in England for two months when Kristallnacht happened.

The night of broken glass. When Nazi officers took to the streets and forcefully evicted, beat up and killed shop owners, breaking their windows and ripping thousands of men from their families and sending them to detention camps, for no other reason than the fact that they were Jewish.

After that, his mother and stepfather's visa application sank under the eddy of millions applying to get out of the country.

Every day he wished he'd been able to force them to follow him. That they had agreed to his plan to smuggle them across the border. They could all be in Switzerland now and safe.

The tide had turned in Germany, and the Nazis were no

longer trying to disguise the sheer hatred they felt for the Jews. Perhaps for the first time people were truly beginning to see how bad things were for people like Sebastien and his family. The trouble was, like all over the world, Britain's Home Office was inundated with requests for visas.

Unlike many countries, Britain opened up their immigration policy, but with so many people needing to get out there was a very long waiting list.

Sadly, there was also a small but growing backlash to their welcome of refugees, with many fearing that the country would be overrun with foreigners who would take their jobs. It wasn't true. The numbers coming in were still relatively minor compared to the millions of people who needed help but who had been denied. Soon the only way other Jews like him would be able to enter was with a sponsor and a guaranteed job. Both of which were near impossible to get when you were trying to run for your life.

The train jolted and Sebastien pressed up against an older man by accident, and apologised in his accented English.

'Bloody foreigner,' muttered the old man.

Sebastien didn't react. Unfortunately, he was all too used to how some people just seemed to resent him being there. Heard that tinge of an accent and turned cold. Or found out he was Jewish and became awkward. Most were kind though, and he'd been surprised at that, and grateful. He would have understood if they'd all been like the grumpy passenger.

Anything was better than being in Germany. He could tolerate a few grim looks or turns away when someone moaned that 'they' were coming for their jobs. He didn't get into debates or try to explain that people were being persecuted out of their homes any more. He had in the beginning, but, when he got into an argument that almost turned into a fist-fight with a drunk in a pub, Sebastien realised that he was playing a dangerous game. He could have gone to prison or been deported straight back to the Nazis and none of it would have changed that drunk's mind.

So he focused on what he could control, and that was saving every penny he had to sponsor his family's visas.

Nothing else mattered.

4

Sebastien made his way out into the bitter-cold spring day towards the printing press in Holland Park, a ten-minute walk away, his grey hat tipped forward, his gloveless hands buried deep in his second-hand wool coat, the freezing wind biting his neck.

The air perked him up as he hurried, along with a crowd of similar commuters, women in heels rushing to offices, men in suits, newspapers curled up beneath one arm, briefcases in their hands. The thought of a fresh pot of coffee gave him new life as he made his way to work.

He was halfway through his morning shift when his colleague, Frank, a short, stocky man with a kind smile, who was beginning to bald, brought him his second steaming cup of coffee.

Frank Block was an older man in his mid-fifties who liked to hum when he worked, and, like Sebastien, he was a refugee. He'd left Vienna with his wife and children just after Germany's annexation of Austria with the help of a friend who worked at a Jewish charity. The charity had helped Frank get the job too.

Sebastien had applied to the charity to ask for their help with his family on Frank's recommendation, but they were drowning under the weight of so many similar applications, and he just had to hold out hope that one day he would be reunited with them all.

For now, he was grateful to have Frank, who represented the sum total of his social life.

'I think I love you,' said Sebastien, taking the cup of coffee from the older man gratefully.

'You tease,' said Frank.

The two shared a laugh.

Frank often invited him round to his home for dinner with his family. Sebastien was grateful for him. He was the only friend he'd made since he'd arrived in late August the year before. Some days the loneliness was like a living, breathing shadow that stalked him. He missed his family so much that it felt like a part of him had been cut out. As if he were walking around with only half of his heart.

He missed his country too. But he was familiar with that feeling at least. He'd been missing Germany even when he was standing in its caucus. The things he loved about it had been taken from him inch by inch, by the chisel fists of the Nazis, who sought to destroy all that was progressive and beautiful from the country of his birth.

Sometimes when he thought back to before about how different his life used to be in Berlin, before the laws came into place that effectively made him a third-class citizen in his own country, all the friends he used to have, the trips to the theatre to watch the clever, satirical plays he loved and hoped he might one day write, the long intellectual debates he used to have with colleagues and friends who hadn't been afraid to share a different opinion, the small but wonderful, art-filled flat where he lived, with its view of the river... it felt like another life. Like a dream too.

Now he lived in a boarding house in a tiny room up in the loft where he could touch the walls on either side with his elbows half-bent. His view was of the rubbish bins outside and a bit of old concrete. But it was clean and he could come and go as he chose, and he had more rights in his adopted country than he had in the one he used to call home, so Sebastien didn't mind.

They were adjusting the plates for the local paper when Frank saw the advertisement.

'This is near your end, right down the high street in Notting Hill, they're having auditions at the haberdashery shop,' said the older man with interest.

They didn't often comment on what was in the paper they were setting, unless it was some bit of exciting news.

Sebastien came over to have a look. It didn't seem exactly newsworthy, it was just a bit of guff about a local dramatic society that was starting. 'So?' he said.

'You should join them,' said Frank.

Sebastien laughed aloud. 'Me?'

'Yes, you, Seb. Didn't you tell me how much you loved the theatre and how you wanted to write a play some day?'

Sebastien frowned. 'Was I drunk?'

'Yes.'

Sebastien laughed. 'That explains a lot.'

Frank grinned. 'What do they say, my friend, "in vino veritas"? In wine, there's truth. Look, it's on your one night off from all your jobs.'

Frank thought he worked too much. Why escape one prison to put yourself in another? he often said. He always told Sebastien he thought he should quit the canning factory job, but Sebastien couldn't let himself do that. There was another reason he worked so hard, aside from trying to save up money for his family; working helped him release all the helpless anger he felt.

Last year when Chamberlain had gone to Munich to appease Hitler in his ambitions for the Sudetenland, he was one of the few who secretly hoped they would declare war, so that he might volunteer to fight with the British and could finally do something about all his rage at the Nazis, but nothing had come of that. And now, with Hitler going back on his deal – as Sebastien had known he would – still nothing had happened. How long would it take before the world actually started to take him as a serious threat? How much more was everyone willing to let him get away with? The thought sometimes ate him alive.

Sebastien looked at Frank. He was *serious* about him taking part in this group, and the idea made him burst into laughter. It changed his usual serious expression. Like sunshine on a grey day.

'I get one night off a week – and you think I should go to some haberdashery to audition to become part of some *acting* group?'

Frank nodded. 'Yes,' he said, with a smile. 'A little bit of light-hearted fun is good for the soul, Seb. You're young, you should be with other young people. This is how you'll meet them – by joining things. I was part of a group like this in my university days in Vienna and we had an absolute blast. It beats sitting at home brooding, surely, and eating one of your landlady's offences to cooking?'

Frank had a point. Mrs Bower's idea of cooking was to kill things twice.

Still, Sebastien couldn't believe that the older man was really being serious. 'But I've never acted before.'

'You've written though, it could be a way to get some of that creativity out.'

'As a political journalist! If I'd been creative about it I would have been fired,' Sebastien pointed out.

Frank laughed. 'Well, okay. But you do like the theatre – and small groups like this often stage their own productions. This could be good for you – something else to think about, you know?'

Sebastien didn't answer. He had liked the theatre. He'd loved it really. But then he'd been forbidden from going, like millions of Jews. The person who thought about things like writing plays felt like someone from another life, too.

It seemed almost frivolous now. Even though he knew it probably shouldn't.

'What is happening back home, we have no control over it – you're doing everything you can to help your family. Taking some time to have a little bit of fun, Sebastien, isn't a betrayal, it's the opposite. Knowing there's light gives us strength to face the darkness,' said Frank. 'You have one life, son, you know that better than most, don't let the Nazis keep taking from you. You have a right to all those sides of yourself – especially the lighter ones. They might have forced us not to participate in anything back home, but we shouldn't carry that with us into our new lives. They only win if we let them control us here,' he said, pointing to his head, 'in our minds.'

'You're probably right, Frank, but that still doesn't mean I should join an amateur dramatics group. It feels... silly.'

'What's wrong with that?'

Sebastien stared at him. He was being serious.

'When we were leaving Austria, Seb, the thing that got us through wasn't fear or despair, it was those little moments when the light poured in and we found things funny or silly and remembered who we were. The small inside family jokes that lift the spirits... that bond you closer. When things get tough we need those light moments to remind us that hard things pass too. That there's more to life than white-knuckling your way through it. There is plenty enough time for that. And I'm sure there will be more of that to face before we hear the end of

Hitler, which is why we need something to keep us sane until then. I've known a lot of men turn to drink, especially after the last war, to take the edge off, but there are better ways and you, my friend, need something.'

Sebastien frowned at him.

'Or your face will stay that way.' Frank scrunched his own face to indicate Sebastien's perma-scowl.

Sebastien shot him a mock glare.

The older man laughed. 'If nothing else, go for the biscuits.'

'Biscuits?' said Sebastien in surprise.

Frank nodded. 'There's always biscuits.'

'I don't think so, Frank,' said Sebastien, who wasn't just doubting the promise of biscuits.

Later that evening, when Mrs Bower served Sebastien his dinner, a gristly piece of indeterminate meat with cabbage, he tried his best not to sigh. He cut into it and sampled a tiny bite. It was almost inedible. Sinewy and hard and utterly flavourless. It was little wonder he'd grown so thin.

'Eat up, Mr Raphael, there's seconds if you like.'

The thought made him gag. Thankfully her back was turned. She meant well – unfortunately he regularly had to remind himself of that. 'Thanks Mrs B.'

He'd have to wait for her to leave so that he could make some toast, he thought. But just as that thought cheered him somewhat, there was a knock on the front door. Mrs Bower went to answer it and the sudden noise filling the corridor sounded like a stream of chattering women. He realised, with mounting dread, that she was welcoming the ladies from her sewing group inside.

He froze in horror.

They were doing maintenance at the nearby community hall where the group usually met, and it meant that Mrs Bower was holding their weekly meeting at home now. He'd forgotten that they had changed it to this Thursday instead of the usual Tuesday night when he was blissfully at work at the canning factory. He should have known: that was why the other lodgers had made themselves scarce!

They were a boisterous, interfering lot. They liked to stare at him, like he was some living exhibit. He could probably put up with that, but the questions were worse. So intrusive and repetitive. It was gossip disguised as care. He hadn't minded explaining his situation the first time, but when it became clear that all they were interested in was hearing about the drama of life in a troubled foreign country, ad nauseam, he stopped entertaining them with it. His life wasn't some story, it had been a nightmare, and that nightmare was still how millions of people were living their lives. He stood up, and went to scrape off his plate and make his excuses. Mrs Bower's home wasn't big and the walls were thin. Even if he hid in his bedroom, the peals of laughter and whispers would still carry up the stairs, so he'd have to find somewhere else to spend the next few hours.

He put on his navy, woollen coat, deciding that at the very least he could get himself something else to eat.

Just as he was preparing to go out, though, he saw one of Mrs Bower's guests, Rita Fitzgerald, an attractive woman with bright red curls and enormous, heavily kohled green eyes, pop her head round the living room door and give him a slow smile.

Sebastien was like a deer in the headlights for a moment, until his brain kicked in and he managed to say a quick goodbye and beat a hasty retreat into the cold street, ignoring the way she looked utterly put out. The last time they'd met, a few weeks previously, she'd all but proposed they begin an affair and then laughed at him when he'd seemed genuinely shocked.

'I heard all you foreigners are wild, it's no use playing coy with me, Mr Raphael,' she'd said, when she'd cornered him on the landing outside his room while the others were busy chatting in the living room, her long red nails gently scraping the skin of his neck and making him shiver, and not in a good way.

It was curious, the way some English women seemed to think this of 'foreign' men, Sebastien had thought. They'd be surprised at how conventional many of them actually were.

Sebastien wasn't, necessarily. He wasn't a prude, either, meaningless sexual encounters just didn't interest him. Besides, he'd overheard her saying that she just wanted to get revenge on her husband, Stanley, for his affair with his secretary. Though he sympathised, he didn't feel like being used.

The thought of dealing with her made him feel even more tired.

His dash to freedom took him straight out into the rainy street, where he had to turn the collar of his coat up so that the sudden onslaught of water didn't run down his neck. He realised too late that he'd left his hat behind. There was no chance he was going back for it now, though.

He walked briskly to the bistro on the corner, only to frown as he patted his pockets. In his rush to get out, it wasn't just his hat he'd left behind, he'd forgotten his wallet too. He sighed in frustration, then shuffled back into the rain-lashed street, biting back a curse. He waited for a car to go past, not seeing the puddle near the kerb until the car sprayed most of it onto his trousers. 'Blast!' he cursed, then crossed over to the other side of the road.

Shivering and feeling completely miserable and alone, he was just about to pass a shop that was lit up with light, only to snort in amused recognition when he saw the spools of thread and yarn in the window. He was standing in front of the Thrifty Thimble. The haberdashery from the advertisement that Frank had got so excited about. It was where the auditions for the local amateur dramatics group were being held. The group that Frank thought he should attend.

He was about to walk on when he remembered the biscuits.

He just hoped the older man was right about that.

His stomach rumbled, and he reasoned saying a few lines might not be the worst price to pay to get out of the rain and get something free to eat.

It showed how much he disliked Mrs Bower's sewing group, never mind her cooking, that he was prepared to do just that.

Later on he would wonder if it was more than the promise of biscuits that had actually propelled his feet. If the older man's words about needing something besides his anger to think about had been what truly drove him through the door.

5

LONDON, MARCH 1939

Finley was nervous. The advertisement had been up for a week and tonight was the night of the auditions for her new amateur dramatics group.

So far no one had turned up.

She was beginning to regret the wasted effort of getting her mother's permission to use the haberdashery shop for rehearsals, not to mention opening the good biscuits, when the door chime finally went.

She breathed out a sigh of relief and made her way to the front of the shop, only to slump in disappointment when she saw two women, in their mid-sixties, enter and begin looking at the ribbons and thread with interest.

'Sorry, the shop is closed, we're using the back room for an event tonight.'

She knew she should have put up a sign.

One of the older women straightened and shot Finley a look from above her purple-rimmed spectacles that Finley couldn't help thinking would work rather well on stage.

She had darkly peppered grey hair, and ebony eyes, and was wearing a mauve shawl with some flair.

'Yes, I know. That's why I am here,' she said, raising her chin. Her voice was quite posh, though every now and again they could hear a bit of northern lilt. 'One did theatre in one's youth, you know?'

'Oh, did one?' said her companion, a short, attractive woman of south Asian appearance, who was wearing a green sari. She had a somewhat mischievous smile that was rather infectious.

The other woman sniffed and assured her, 'Yes, one did,' possibly not getting the joke. Not to mention the bad grammar.

The woman in the sari bit back a grin as she came forward. 'I am Sunella Singh. I am here because when my son and I saw your advertisement, I mentioned that I had always thought joining an amateur dramatics group would be fun... and he was foolish enough to bet me that I wouldn't have the guts to audition.

'I ask you, how can a child not know its own parent like that? I *love* a challenge. It's not like I was some ordinary house-wife, no offence,' she went on, looking at the other woman, 'I was one of the first female surgeons in India.'

'I beg your pardon,' said the other woman.

'A surgeon,' said Sunella slowly, as if the other woman was a bit dim or hard of hearing.

'Not that! I was taking about your presumption that I was a housewife!'

'Oh, I'm sorry!'

'As it happens I am a housewife, most women are, but that doesn't mean you should just assume it.'

'But why, if most are?'

'Because it's rude.'

'It's rude to point out the obvious?'

'You know what is obvious—?'

Finley looked from one to the other awkwardly, then dived

in, hoping to avoid an argument. 'I'm Prudence Finley, but everyone just calls me Finley.'

'Anita Hardglass,' said the woman with the mauve shawl, who looked a bit like a kettle that was starting to steam.

'Are you two friends?' asked Finley.

'Absolutely not,' said Anita, still simmering.

Sunella raised a brow, 'I'm not sure the "absolutely" was necessary. But no, never met her in my life till now,' she said. Something about the way she said it seemed to imply that this wasn't necessarily a bad thing.

'Oh, erm, well. Come in, come in,' said Finley, showing them to the back room, where she had set up some chairs, along with a table, which housed the aforementioned biscuits, cordial, a jug of water and some glasses, as well as several copies of the play she was using for the auditions, *Romeo and Juliet*.

Finley was beginning to think that maybe she should have chosen something a little more age-appropriate when the door chime went again and an older gentleman, perhaps in his sixties or seventies, came inside, shaking out his umbrella. He was tall and thin, with a long, crooked nose, silvery hair and sparkling blue eyes. Beneath his chin was a red and green checked scarf that looked rather dapper on him. She liked him immediately. 'Is this fair Verona, where we lay our scene?' he asked. Despite his confident words, Finley could detect a slight catch of apprehension in his voice.

'What?' asked Anita. 'You're in Notting Hill.'

'No, I meant...' he said, suddenly bashful, and it was quite clear he was forcing his bravado, '...never mind.'

'It is,' said Finley, with a wide smile. 'It seems we've found at least one pair of star-crossed lovers already,' she added.

The older man laughed nervously as he eyed the other two women as if he had found himself in a river with piranhas. 'Indeed.'

'I'm Finley, this is Anita and Sunella,' she said, indicating the other women.

'A-Archie Greeves,' he stuttered.

'Nice to meet you,' said Finley.

Then she looked at the chunky gold watch on the inside of her wrist. It was her father's. It had been sent back to them after he died in France during the Great War, in 1918. Finley had been utterly touched when her mother gave it to her for her sixteenth birthday, along with the pearl earrings she always wore. She always thought her father's watch would go to Christopher, but her mother had surprised her by saying that she thought he would have wanted her to have it. She had been his *little chip*, her mother had reminded her; he'd called her that because she was a bit of a chip off the old block.

On the back her mother had had inscribed her father's motto *Do nothing small, least of all life!* The watch itself was big and gold and dominated her wrist, but she loved it.

It was one of those strange but lovely little idiosyncrasies of her mother's; though she desperately wanted Finley to be more practical, and would have been thrilled if her daughter wanted a more conventional life, she also didn't want to stand in the way of her dreams. Perhaps that was what love was. Hope that someone might succeed but fear that life might crush them along the way.

Her mother might have grumbled, but she'd agreed to let Finley use the shop's back room for her new group, and she'd wished her luck too.

Finley saw that it was quarter to seven, and thought they should probably get started soon. 'Shall we give it another five minutes, then begin the auditions? There's some blackberry cordial, and please help yourself to the biscuits,' she told them.

'When will we find out if we're in the group?' asked Anita, who was clearly not the kind to waste time, or mince words for that matter. 'Will it be straight after we audition or will you ring or write to us to let us know?'

'I will let you know after your audition,' Finley confirmed. She despised waiting for callbacks. The thought of turning anyone down in person filled her with dread, though.

She was also regretting not getting started straight away, as everyone stood around awkwardly sipping cordial for a few minutes, and no one else arrived. She couldn't help worrying that it would make it harder to reject anyone if she had got to know them all first...

After a few pained minutes more, Finley had to face the fact that the only people who looked like they wanted to join the group were of retirement age. Oh well, she thought, with her typical, can't-be-down-for-long attitude, at least it meant they'd likely be free for rehearsals.

She brightened at that thought. 'Right, gang, I think we should get started,' she called, trying to salvage together some practicality. 'Sunella, if you can read the part of the nurse, please?'

Sunella looked put out. 'But I have prepared Juliet. You said we should prepare a part in the advertisement.'

There was a loud tut from Anita.

'What?' said Sunella, looking at the older woman, whose face didn't attempt to hide her scorn. 'You don't think someone like me should play Juliet?'

'No, I don't,' said Anita, raising a brow. 'Not unless we're doing a pantomime, and if we are, well, count me out. Juliet is meant to be a young girl. Not a grandmother!'

Finley held up a hand in a placating gesture. 'It doesn't matter, we are just using this play for the auditions,' she said, hoping to keep the peace, 'and you are completely right, I did ask you to prepare something. I forgot. Let's begin, go ahead, Juliet.'

Sunella shot Anita a victorious look, then took a deep breath and somehow before their eyes seemed to transform into a young girl who had just fallen in love for the first time.

Finley blinked. She was good. Raw, but that could be developed and nurtured. Maybe this could actually work, she thought with an enormous sense of relief.

As a result, when Sunella finished Finley exclaimed, 'Oh well done!' and clapped perhaps a bit too enthusiastically.

'It was all right?' asked Sunella, looking uncharacteristically nervous.

'It was definitely all right. More than,' said Finley, grinning widely.

Sunella beamed at them. 'I can't wait to tell Rajesh.' She giggled, and turned to leave the room.

'Wait – where are you going?' asked Finley, her mouth falling open in surprise.

Sunella turned back slowly, a confused look on her face. 'Oh, I...'

Finley frowned. 'Don't you want to join the group?'

'You want me to join?'

'Of course.'

Sunella looked stunned.

Anita did too. 'You can't be serious, you're going to make her Juliet?'

Finley sighed. 'Anita, as I've said already said, we haven't decided on the play we will be doing just yet, *Romeo and Juliet* is just for the auditions.'

She turned to Sunella. 'I would love it if you joined the group.'

Sunella looked wrong-footed. 'Well, the thing is, I just told my son I would audition to prove to him that I could. I'm not sure about joining another group. I've had a few bad experiences,' she admitted, then grimaced. 'The history club I was in? Well, they *said* they wanted us to share our thoughts, but then when I did, particularly on the British and India, they said I was perhaps being a bit too honest, and the same thing happened with the WI. I mean, not the exact same thing, well, maybe a little... I mean for a country who colonised another for over a hundred years, calling it the "jewel in their crown", you'd think they would have at least known that curry was a plant...'

Finley snorted. She had a point.

'I can just imagine,' said Archie.

Sunella looked at him in surprise, and he began to stutter. 'I-I only meant I can imagine the type. The history club where only one pen writes the story... not to mention the kind of Brit who goes abroad yet somehow never leaves home at the same time. Neighbours of ours stayed in a villa in Italy for a few months, and when I suggested they hire a local woman as a cook, to get a real flavour of the cuisine, they were genuinely shocked at the idea of trying foreign food.' He snorted.

Sunella laughed. 'I think that happens everywhere, really – I have family members who won't try British food, even though they've lived here since the end of the last war, and, I mean, cream tea is food of the gods.'

Archie grinned in return. 'You're not wrong.'

Finley said, 'I'd like for this group to be a welcoming place for everyone, a place for all opinions and for trying new things. Also,' she added with a cheeky grin, 'I for one will never object to spices if you ever want to bring round some nibbles.' She grinned, giving Sunella a wide smile. Finley loved trying new things.

Archie nodded. 'Seconded, well, if I get in that is.'

Sunella stared back, undecided, for a moment, then her face broke out into a mischievous smile. 'Well, if for no other reason than to absolutely shock Rajesh, all right.'

'Excellent,' said Finley, bouncing on the balls of her feet. Sunella took a seat.

Anita's audition was up next. She had prepared the part of Juliet's mother. Where Sunella had been raw, Anita had done some acting before, and it showed. She knew how to hold herself, where to stand, and how to control her breathing and use her voice so that it carried across the room. She also delivered some spectacularly withering looks.

'You're in, definitely,' said Finley. Anita nodded and took a seat. It wasn't a surprise to her.

Finley realised that, seeing as so few people had turned up, unless the older man was truly awful she would most likely have to take him too.

'Once more unto the breach,' said Archie, loftily, though really it did look as if he were facing a battle. As he began it soon became apparent that it was, alas one he was losing, as he began bungling Mercutio's speech rather dreadfully.

His voice went thin and high yet somehow also quite monotonous, and he ended with a rather feeble plea on the 'a plague on both your houses' bit. They could see his hands shaking horribly. Finley winced.

He was terrible.

Archie closed his eyes, shook his head, then rubbed his hands against his trousers. 'C-can I go again? S-sorry about this,' he stammered. 'I'm not sure why I'm so nervous... only it's been about forty years since I did anything like this.'

'Absolutely,' said Finley, swallowing, 'take your time, it'll come back, I'm sure,' she caught sight of Anita who was staring at him like he was something beneath her shoes and was able to take a good guess at the source of the poor man's nerves. She hoped it was just nerves. She really liked him. She knew that it should have been more about talent, but she hated the idea of asking him not to join.

He went again.

He was worse, if anything. His nerves were still very apparent, he was too fast, still rather monotonous and lacking any emotion (apart from his all-too-evident fear). Finley felt awful for him. It was odd because when he wasn't trying to perform he had such *flair*. Perhaps there was some potential there, buried beneath the nerves... buried rather deep, that was. Well, she hoped so anyway. She bit her lip as she blinked up at him. She'd asked for naturals though. She wanted to put on a play rather soon, one that she could perform at All the World's a Stage so that she could finally get out of the horrible career slump she was in and get her big break. Having someone like Archie in her amateur dramatics group would mean that they would need a lot more time to be anywhere near ready for her to put on a production.

What she should do, of course, was to politely decline him. This was meant to be a group going places... and the only place she'd get with someone like this would be further backward.

She opened her mouth to do it. She knew she *should*. Only to frown.

Is this who you want to be, Prudence Finley? she asked herself. *Someone who only takes the easy route to success?* Since when had she ever given up on something or someone because it would involve hard work? Since when had she ever been accused of being sensible, for that matter? Hadn't she learned how to tap-dance for a musical in two weeks even though Lord knew she had two left feet? Hadn't she learned a Birmingham accent for a role by working in a cotton factory for a month?

If she said she was going to be a director then this was her job, wasn't it? To not only direct, but coach and train? Wasn't that why she'd said she didn't just need professionals?

Oh, why didn't I insist on professionals! Why can't I ever be sensible?

No, she reminded herself, firmly, this was meant to be an amateur production, and well, it stood to reason, it wasn't just Finley who would benefit from it; while she had conceived of the idea of the group for purely selfish reasons – to launch her career from it and get talent-spotted – it didn't mean she couldn't also help others in the process. Besides, it might be fun, she thought. To use all she'd learned over the years to encourage them. She knew of exercises that could help

Archie. Wouldn't it be wonderful to see him come out of his shell?

For a long time acting hadn't actually been that fun, if she were honest with herself... She'd been so focused on getting a lead part, some of the joy she used to feel in the beginning had dimmed a little. Well, there was no reason this couldn't reignite some of that old magic along the way. By sharing what she had learned.

Just the thought of all the methods she could use to help Archie fired her up in a way she hadn't expected. She had thought that this group might help her get ahead, but she hadn't considered that she might also enjoy the challenge.

'You're in,' she told Archie.

'Really?' scoffed Anita, and then muttered, 'ridiculous,' under her breath.

Finley ignored her. Sometimes not being sensible *was* the good idea.

'Good. Well, if that's everyone, perhaps we can begin to get to know one another a bit more—'

Just then the bell chimed again. Whoever it was was now rather late. But as no one came through to the back room, she got up to investigate. 'I'll just see who that is,' she said. 'One moment.'

When she got there, though, she stopped in surprise. It was raining heavily outside. Standing in the door of the shop was a tall man, with dark hair and impossibly blue eyes. When she looked at them she frowned, and couldn't help thinking they were the saddest eyes she had ever seen. Until his lips quirked into an apologetic smile as water dripped from his black hair to his black coat and onto the tiled floor. He looked as if he'd just climbed out of the Thames.

But that wasn't what made her catch her breath. It was the fact that he was quite possibly the most handsome man she'd ever seen in her life.

6

As water continued to pool onto the black and white floor tiles, his vivid blue eyes were full of apology as they stared at the floor then back at Finley.

'I-I'm sorry, it was raining frogs and bats and I got caught.'

She was surprised. He had a soft-spoken German accent that was very pleasant. As was the accompanying even smile.

'Cats and dogs, you mean?' she said, gently teasing him, and then cursing herself.

He closed his eyes for a second, then laughed in embarrassment. 'Yes, sorry. Is that what they say?'

She grinned. 'Yes, but I prefer yours. More, erm, logical maybe – as they could come out of the sky and ground.'

'Logical, yes, that's what I was going for,' he joked, giving her a wider smile. He'd been handsome before but now he was devastating. It was a bit much in such a small room and Finley felt flustered.

She blushed when she realised she was staring.

'Oh, um. My mother keeps some towels behind the counter, let me get you one,' she said, then went to find the basket of rolled-up towels that were kept precisely for when customers arrived in the pristine shop bringing the weather inside with them.

'Here,' she said, holding out a towel.

Up close he had a clean soap smell, mixed with sandal-wood. She stopped herself from leaning forward to breathe it in.

He was about to bend down and use it on the floor when she laughed. 'Use it on yourself, silly.'

He laughed too. 'Oh, thanks.'

Finley caught herself staring once more. She looked away, then swallowed. 'We're back through here,' she said. 'You're here for the drama group?'

'Oh... erm, yes.' He seemed to be hesitating now that he was here.

'Come on through to the back,' she said, and waited for him by the entrance.

As he walked through, Sunella gave a low whistle.

'Don't do that,' admonished Anita. 'We are professionals.'

'Sorry, but...' she said, gesturing towards Sebastien with a set of very wide eyes. 'I can't be the only one who is happy we're not just going to be a seniors' club.'

'He still has to audition,' Anita reminded her. 'But yes, me too,' she whispered.

Archie made a tutting sound, but he winked to show he was only kidding.

'Erm,' said Sebastien, who looked a bit like a deer in the headlights.

'Come in, I won't let them bite,' said Finley, then introduced herself properly as well as the others.

'Sebastien Raphael,' he said.

'What a beautiful name,' said Archie, voicing just what Finley had been thinking herself. 'Jewish?'

Sebastien nodded. He appeared to tense, like he was waiting for them to ask him questions about that.

'Good to have you here,' said Archie.

'Yes,' agreed Finley.

'So you're a refugee?' asked Anita.

Sebastien frowned. 'Yes.'

Finley cringed, then mouthed 'sorry' at Sebastien.

'Thanks,' he said, and the grateful look he gave her made her breath catch.

'Do you have a copy of the play?' asked Finley, jumping in in case Anita decided to ask the poor man any questions about his life.

Sebastien shook his head.

'That's fine.'

As Finley passed him one, their fingers touched for a second, and her stomach did a small flip when their eyes met.

'I haven't prepared anything,' he whispered.

'Why don't you read from the part where Romeo first meets Juliet?' suggested Sunella, giving Finley a wink that she did *not* appreciate.

Archie stifled a laugh, as did Sunella. Finley shot them both a quelling look.

'I don't know why that's funny, he's the obvious choice if Finley is going to be Juliet,' said Anita, huffily.

Finley had to stop herself from rolling her eyes. 'Like I said earlier, it's not decided what play we will eventually perform, we're just reading from *Romeo and Juliet* tonight for the auditions.'

'Right,' said Sunella. 'She's said that a few times now.'

'Has she?' said Anita.

Finley closed her eyes for a moment, realising she would have to learn to practise patience thanks to Anita. 'Why don't you try from the balcony scene?' she asked Sebastien. He nodded. Then flipped through the script until he was at the right moment and then began to perform. He was nervous at first, and a little embarrassed and clearly self-conscious to be reading the famous scene, but his voice was rich and, when he delivered the line about wishing he were a glove on Juliet's hand so that he might touch her cheek, the look of longing on his face felt very real, and Finley wasn't the only one who thought he definitely had something. She found it hard to tear her eyes away from him, and for just a moment she knew exactly how Romeo felt.

'Um. That's good, thanks Sebastien,' she said when he'd finished.

'Wow,' said Sunella.

'So compelling,' said Archie.

'Not totally without merit,' admitted Anita.

'Erm, thank you for your time,' he said and, like Sunella, seemed to be getting ready to leave. His eyes strayed longingly for a moment to Finley, then to the table with the drinks and biscuits.

Finley stood up hastily. He couldn't leave. She had the irrational urge to rush over to him but she resisted. 'Don't go! I mean, you're in. Help yourself to a drink, there's some biscuits too.'

'Er, okay,' he said, hesitating, then going over to the snack table, where he helped himself to a couple of ginger biscuits.

'Help yourselves too, everyone, and we can have a bit of a chat about next steps.'

Anita made no move to get any refreshments. Her gaze fixed Finley firmly to the spot. It was one of disbelief.

Finley frowned. 'You don't want to get something to drink?'

'Were you always just going to take all of us?' Anita asked, scornfully, 'considering you haven't said no to anyone tonight. Even when maybe you should have,' she added, glancing at Archie meaningfully.

Archie looked at the floor. He'd clearly got what she meant. Finley saw his hands shake as he reached for a glass, and felt a surge of anger.

'We could have avoided all this fuss, then,' said Anita.

Finley frowned. 'I think we just got lucky,' she said, diplomatically, which seemed to go down rather well. 'We will have to work hard but I think it will be worth it.'

Archie gave her a small appreciative smile at that.

'I can't believe I've joined my first ever drama group,' said Sunella, brightly. 'I've always wanted to learn how to act, and to learn from a professional like Finley, well, that's exciting.'

'I think so too,' said Archie.

Finley felt touched by their comments. 'I'm excited too,' she said, and found that she meant it. It would be wonderful to have something besides the state of the world at present to think about, something positive and perhaps a bit fun. She wondered if the others felt the same.

She couldn't help but wonder at what had brought Sebastien here. What his story was. Anita had guessed that he was a refugee. Finley had been struck by the sadness in his eyes when they'd met in the front of the shop.

Part of her couldn't help wishing she could do something to take that pain from him. She wasn't sure how though.

Mentally she shook herself, reminding herself to be a professional. That wasn't why he was here. Though it seemed from the way he'd sounded so unsure of joining them as if he'd almost stumbled inside by mistake... but he had been aware of what they were doing, so maybe there was another reason as to why he'd wanted to leave. She hoped he'd stay. And not just because they needed his talent. She wanted to get to know him.

She blew her cheeks out, hoping this wasn't going to be a problem. She didn't need the distraction, she reminded herself. She had a plan.

'Let's begin by getting to know each other a little and then we can discuss the play we will perform together. I'm thinking maybe Chekhov or Shaw? If all goes well, we might even get to have our first performance on stage at All the World's a Stage pub.'

Anita gasped. 'Really?'

When Sunella looked confused, Archie explained, 'That's pretty much a professional venue.'

Sebastien started to choke on a biscuit. He looked at Finley in shock. Archie leapt forward to help and Sebastien held up a hand to say he was fine, but he did look utterly wrong-footed.

'Do you really think we could manage that, Miss Finley?' asked Anita.

'It's just Finley, please. Even my mother calls me by our surname, it's a long story. And I don't see why not.'

'Really?' said Archie, in a small voice. He looked terrified at the prospect, his eyes wide. 'From what I have heard they only take quite seasoned groups?'

'If we work hard, I see no reason we can't.'

They still did not seem convinced. 'I know the manager,' Finley admitted, at last.

'Well, that helps,' said Sunella.

Finley shrugged. She only hoped it *would* help. She hadn't exactly spoken to Simon about it just yet. At the thought of her ex, she felt a sudden rush of nerves. She hoped he would agree.

Sebastien was experiencing a storm of mixed emotions.

Discomfort and shame at the fact that he was likely wasting their time by actually agreeing to be a part of a group he had no intention of really joining, but also something else, something he knew he might have to examine later, a wish that things could be different. That he could just be someone who had come here to join what looked like it could actually be something fun.

He thought he'd stay for a bit longer and then try to find a way to leave. He hadn't counted on actually being invited to join them. As they all excitedly began to talk about putting on a play in this well-known pub in the theatre district, he felt like a heel.

When they started to share their stories with one another, he squirmed. He'd let this go on long enough; he did not want to share his life story with them – he had seen how the air had suddenly changed when he'd said that he was Jewish. And when Anita had asked him if he was a refugee.

But then there was Finley. It was her more than anything that had stopped his feet, turning them to lead at the thought of leaving behind that smile. He couldn't remember the last time a woman had appeared to look into his soul like that. If it had ever happened.

When she spoke her eyes lit up, and she had a way of speaking that meant even the most ordinary of things felt like they fizzed with fun. It was like looking in a reverse mirror, and he saw, reflected in her warm amber eyes, his own despair. His ever-present loneliness. Maybe Frank had been right. And not just about the biscuits, he thought, as he helped himself to another one.

Maybe it wouldn't be the worst idea in the world to make a friend.

Finley started them off. 'So, I'm Finley, I'm twenty-eight and an assistant costumer for the Glory Theatre. I also work as a coat-check girl for a jazz club in Soho called Smooth Cafe, one of two things that cause my mother's headaches – the other being the fact that I am also a semi-professional actress,' she said, waggling her eyebrows theatrically.

Sebastien couldn't help but grin.

There was a catcall from Archie.

'Thank you,' Finley said with a grin. 'Anita, you go next.'

'All right, I am Anita Hardglass, I trained as a mathematics teacher, before I had Tim—' she broke off, frowning. For just a moment her face looked utterly haunted and a flash of sadness made her look vulnerable, before it was replaced by her usual stern demeanour.

'...became a housewife,' she amended, shooting Sunella a look for her earlier quip about housewives. 'I was part of the drama club in my high school, and I would have trained as an actress if my parents hadn't insisted on me going into teaching.'

This caused a bit of a hubbub, as it turned out quite a few parents had done similar things. Finley told them about how her mother mentioned that there was still time to become a trained secretary every week; and Archie had a similar story of his own.

'I wanted to study literature, and be a writer, but all the men in my family were lawyers, so that's what I became until I retired, then I retrained as a librarian. Thankfully by then my parents weren't there to witness it but my brother does insist they are turning in their graves.'

They all had a good laugh at that.

Sebastien hadn't found the right moment to leave, so reluctantly he said, 'I'm Sebastien Raphael, I was born in Berlin, where I was a journalist for a number of years, but now I work at a printing press.'

He prepared himself for the questions but the ones that came surprised him.

'I went to Berlin, years ago, before those awful thugs took over, such a beautiful city,' said Archie.

'Do you miss writing?' asked Finley.

Sebastien looked at her, a bit surprised. No one ever asked him that.

'Sometimes.'

The truth was, he did. But life had taken a bite out of him and he'd lost his fire along the way. He'd written to a few papers in England but he hadn't been persistent enough, not like he used to be in his former life, if he were honest with himself. He'd been too focused on surviving, finding a place to live, paying his bills and trying to get by; sometimes the person he was felt like a memory. He wanted to find him again. Part of him knew it would be how he could really discharge the pent-up anger he felt – writing would make him feel useful again, like he was making a difference – but the other, larger part of himself that had taken over his day-to-day life was still trying to catch his breath.

He didn't know how to share that, though, and wouldn't have even if he could. It had been one thing writing about political events close to home; it would be quite another speaking and writing about his own experiences. Also, he wasn't sure they would understand.

'Do you have family still in Berlin?' asked Anita.

He was starting to feel like an exhibit – exactly what he'd hoped to avoid tonight.

'Yes.'

Anita nodded. 'And are they also—?'

'Jewish, yes,' he said, shifting in his chair. Knowing that this was what she was asking. 'Yes.' Then anticipating the next question, he said, 'There is a long waiting list for obtaining a visa.'

'I hope they're able to join you soon,' said Finley.

'Thanks.'

Finley saw how uncomfortable he was starting to look, and she felt a stab of empathy. She couldn't even imagine what he must have been going through being in a foreign country, separated from his loved ones and not knowing if things were going to get worse.

So she changed the subject. 'Do Thursday nights suit everyone at around the same time? Or would Wednesdays be better?' she asked.

'I don't mind,' said Anita and Sunella together.

'Makes no difference to me,' said Archie.

'Sebastien,' said Finley, 'do you have a preference?'

Sebastien had stood up, about to leave. The night had been better than he would have expected, but honestly he had no intention of actually joining the group at all.

But Finley was putting him on the spot. There was something so warm and sunny about her. When he'd seen her there in the shop, smiling at him, for just a moment he had felt himself wondering what it might be like to come home and be greeted like that. Imagined a new life for himself rather than the day-to-day limbo he was still in without his family...

The truth was he was utterly lonely, and he hadn't realised that was what had been eating him alive for so long until right then. He'd been too tired to think of himself, so focused on helping his family that it wasn't until he caught himself having this ordinary but lovely moment with this girl that he realised it.

They were complete strangers, but she had a way of making people feel at home. Like they were the only ones in the room. And it was hard to not want to be around that. Every time she spoke to him, he felt himself inching closer, as if to a fire.

Her warm brown eyes were staring at him so expectantly and he didn't really know how to tell her he wasn't coming back. That this was a mistake. Perhaps a part of him wanted to, if only just to see her again, he admitted to himself, as he found himself saying, 'Um, well, Thursday is my only night off,' instead of what he had meant to say which was that he really didn't have the time or energy to join a group like this. Or that despite what Frank had said it did feel silly to join an amateur dramatics group, after everything he'd just been through. They might all be in the same room but they were in different worlds.

'Thursday it is,' said Finley, bouncing on the balls of her feet and clapping her hands excitedly. Her dark curls danced on her shoulders, catching the light, turning auburn. She had the kind of face that grew more beautiful the more you got to know the person inside, he realised. Then felt an ache, as he realised how much he wanted someone in his life.

'I'll see you all next week.'

As everyone said their goodbyes, he took a step forward towards her, without realising.

'Er, actually,' he said, touching her hand, only to get a small jolt.

They both laughed a little nervously.

'What is it?' she asked.

Sebastien blinked. Up close there were small flecks of green in her eyes. He gave himself a mental push. He would have to be honest with her. Maybe ask for her number, instead of actually joining this group. But for some reason he was finding it difficult. Sebastien couldn't remember the last time he'd gone on a date. It was a lifetime ago. It had been a long time since anyone had looked at him the way she was at that moment, and he was finding it hard not to linger near her. It wasn't like him. Usually he found it far too easy to keep his distance. There was good reason for that, he reminded himself. He had a lot to focus on. But now all he wanted to do was stay near her.

'Um, the thing is, no look, I don't want to make trouble for anyone. I'm not sure if joining is actually a good idea, I mean I don't have any experience.'

'Oh no, please don't worry about that, you're so wonderful,' said Finley, only to blush slightly. 'I mean, your performance was wonderful, you've really got something, Sebastien, it would be a real pity if you didn't give yourself a chance to see what you could do. I think you're probably a bit like Sunella, a real natural.'

He couldn't help feeling moved by that.

Finley continued. 'Besides, we desperately need you.' She was whispering, there was an infectious quality to her voice. 'I mean, it's not like Archie could have been Romeo – you have no idea how happy I am that you came through that door,' she said. 'Promise you'll be here next week?' For a second he forgot to breathe.

He stared at her for a beat too long and before he knew what he was doing he was agreeing.

7

KOBLENZ, APRIL 1939

Twelve-year-old Katrin Raphael was excited.

She was with her best friend Sami and they had taken the train to the town of Koblenz to see the latest film with Bing Crosby. It was supposed to have been a bit cut down by the censorship process the Nazis applied to American films, cutting out bits that they objected to, but at least they could still watch it.

They'd both told their parents that they were going to each other's houses that Saturday morning to work on a project. The journey from Rüdesheim to Koblenz was just over an hour and it felt a bit like she was going to a big city, considering how small Rüdesheim was.

It had been so long since she'd been to the cinema. She'd practically been a little kid the last time. Her parents refused to take the risk, even though, according to Sami, everyone did it.

She knew she would have to keep it secret though. Not only would her parents be furious if they found out she was breaking at least three rules – lying, going to Koblenz, seeing a film that was a perhaps a bit mature... what they were doing was, technically, illegal.

Jews weren't allowed to go to the cinema.

But Sami knew of a cinema where they didn't bother to check documentation. She did it all the time with her sisters, apparently.

Katrin knew she would be in trouble if her parents found out, but, really, there was more to life, wasn't there, than just never having any fun at all?

Home wasn't a fun place to be. Everything was so tense. Her mother had lost so much weight and had deep circles beneath her eyes and Katrin thought she probably didn't sleep much. Her father Gunther was the same gentle soul but with Sebastien away it was like the light had gone.

He used to bring the joy whenever he came to visit, making the long journey from Berlin every few weeks. They would go for long walks or picnics as a family and it hardly seemed to matter that they couldn't go to the cinema or the theatre.

Now, as Katrin and Sami talked excitedly in the last train carriage, they didn't see the tall woman with reddish-blond hair and freckles take a seat behind them, but she saw them, and she seemed shocked, her mouth set in a firm hard line.

The air was crisp and cool, the sky blue and the air full of the scent of coffee from the café on the corner as they made their way from the train station to the small cinema in the centre of town. Katrin was nervous and, despite all her bravado, when they approached the man dispensing the tickets she held her breath.

He was maybe a bit older than them, in his late teens probably, with light-brown hair and muddy green eyes that didn't bother to look at them properly before he handed them two ticket stubs and told them to use the door on the left.

Katrin had to swallow her glee.

A few minutes later, they made their way to their seats.

Katrin finally relaxed. Sami was right. No one had asked if she was allowed to be there. Her friend was a genius.

As the lights dimmed and the music began to swell, she took a sherbet lemon from Sami, who had bought a bag of sweets from the sweet shop en route, and she wiggled in her seat in excitement.

But it wasn't to last.

A shadow fell over her, and when she looked up there was a man, dressed in a suit, not bothering to lower his voice as he said, 'Jews are not allowed in this cinema, young ladies, come with me!'

Sami and Katrin looked at each other in sinking horror. Katrin's heart thundered in her chest. Everyone was turning to stare. Katrin felt the world beginning to spin.

Behind the loud man was the usher, who was cowering next to a woman with a very familiar face.

It was Elke.

Her mother's best friend.

Ten minutes later, Elke was telling the manager that he didn't need to call the police just yet.

Katrin thought she might be sick.

They'd been shuffled into an office and she and Sami had had to listen as he berated the usher for five minutes, telling him that his carelessness could result in them losing the cinema if the Nazis found out. It was as if she and Sami were contagious. She swallowed. Maybe her parents had been right to be this worried.

Meanwhile, Elke fixed the manager with a small smile, and patted her reddish-blond chignon. Her freckled face was flushed with some deep emotion. 'I used to work with her mother, and we were friendly. I will take the girls home and explain the situation. No one needs to know.'

Katrin frowned. Elke was making out as if she barely knew her mother, instead of being her closest friend. Did she not want the manager to know that? Was she embarrassed that her best friend was a Jew?

'But what if someone reports what happened?' said the manager with a frown.

'I am sure they all believe you have dealt with this appropriately. My husband is a senior officer in the party, and if I believed that this establishment, that I regularly frequent,' she added, meaningfully, 'wasn't taking the matter seriously I would of course intervene, but in this case I'm sure this was a first offense, correct?'

He frowned. 'Is it a first offense?' he asked, looking at the girls, then at the usher, and daring them to say otherwise.

They all nodded hastily.

As the manager's hand strayed towards the phone, Elke said, 'It's up to you, of course, but they are children, and they didn't actually see the film, so perhaps having them leave with a warning would be the best scenario – no need to get the *party* involved...'

He paled. Katrin could see his Adam's apple bob as he swallowed. 'No need. Young ladies, if we catch you here again the police will be called to you, understand?'

They nodded fast.

The train ride home wasn't nearly as fun as the one into Koblenz.

Katrin endured Elke's lecture while Sami cried.

Katrin stared out the window, a frown on her face, when they finally left the train station and Elke saw her to her front door, saying that she would need to have a word with her mother. She raced upstairs to her room and slammed the door, finally releasing the anger that had been brewing slowly since Elke had informed on her, in hot, angry, tears.

Her parents came inside a few minutes later and lay down next to her, their arms around her.

'I'm so sorry, my darling,' said her mother, her voice sounding broken-hearted.

Katrin finally looked up from her soaked pillow. 'Why are you sorry?' she sobbed. 'I was the one who went.'

Her father swore loudly.

She blinked at him in surprise. There were tears in his eyes, and she realised his anger was really fear.

'Darling, it was wrong of you to lie to us, and for you to go to the cinema without asking. It was stupid, so stupid of you to put yourself at risk like that!'

She sat up. 'I'm stupid?' she hissed.

'You acted stupidly, yes, Katrin. You know how dangerous things are at the moment. You know you shouldn't have gone.'

She shook her head, violently. '*No!*'

They looked shocked.

'The way that – that man looked at us, it was as if we were lepers or something. Like you could catch something from us. It's nonsense! No one should get to tell another human being that they aren't allowed to go somewhere because of how they were born.'

Her lips quivered, and more angry tears spilled over. 'Elke tried to tell me the whole way home that I must be smart. That I must "think", and I understand what she was trying to tell me and what you're trying to tell me too. But I refuse to let anyone make me believe that this was *right*.' She raised her chin, which wobbled slightly. 'Maybe it is stupid of me, but I feel like I should go back next week just to show them that – to prove that they don't have the right to make me feel that I'm worth less than them just because I'm a Jew!'

'Katrin,' gasped her father, shocked.

'Promise me you won't actually do that!' cried her mother, horrified.

Katrin wiped away another angry tear. She stared at them both for a long moment. They looked petrified.

'Fine, I won't go back. But I will *never* believe that what Elke did was smart. Or that she was trying to teach me a hard lesson out of a place of "love". She might have really been worried about me but that's only because deep down she probably does think I don't actually *deserve* to be at that cinema.'

Her mother opened her mouth as if she were about to disagree, but she didn't say anything, and Katrin continued.

'She made a choice today, she could have waited for me, and then warned me against going back or threatened to tell you – but she made a scene instead. She said she did that to scare me. It did. But not for the reason she thinks. It scared me to think that a friend could do that. It scared me that she wanted me to believe that I had no right to be there. I will NEVER believe that – I'm sorry about lying to you and I'm sorry for making you worry and I do promise not to go only because I don't want to cause you pain, but I can't be sorry about breaking a rule that shouldn't exist. I'll really be stupid if I start believing that anything they are doing is right.'

8

LONDON, APRIL 1939

It was a cold, blustery spring day, with the rain beginning to fall. The street had mostly emptied when Finley ran into Simon on Shaftesbury Avenue.

He had dark-blond hair, bright-green eyes, and an infectious smile that showed a dimple in his cheek, which at one time she had found irresistible.

'Fin!' he cried, hurrying over on his long legs, looking dapper in a blue suit and matching hat. His eyes shining as he gazed down at her. A half smile on his face.

He was a welcome sight. 'Simon, you are the good cheer I need!'

He pulled a face. 'Ah no, what's happened? What can I do to help?' he said, crooking an elbow for her to take. The dimple appeared. 'Do you have time for a restorative tea or something a bit stronger?'

She nodded. She was on her way home but she had time.

'Tea will be good,' she said. 'It was a chat I had with my brother, Christopher, about the conscription,' she went on with a sigh. 'Naturally he was delighted. My mother was inconsolable all day.'

'Oh Fin, I'm sorry.'

Ever since Hitler had gone back on his agreement not to invade the Czech territories following the Munich Agreement, Britain and France had begun to feel certain that his ambition to dominate Europe was something that needed to be curbed, by force if necessary, and both countries had started to prepare their militaries. For the first time in British history, peacetime conscription had begun.

Thankfully, the current political climate was still against war. Finley held on to that hope as much as she could.

The news though was full of where the outbreak would likely be if it ever happened. Poland. The creation of an independent city state after the last war had been a source of resentment for Germany for years as the former German city of Danzig had become a major port. Hitler had ordered preparations for an invasion and many were on tenterhooks for when that might happen.

If it did, there could be no mistaking that Britain and France would be forced to declare war on Germany.

She prayed that wouldn't happen.

And that her little brother would not be conscripted. So far it hadn't happened. But she was beginning to lose faith that he wouldn't actually volunteer if it came down to it.

They made their way to a tea shop round the corner, and ordered a pot of Earl Grey and a Victoria sponge to share.

'Actually,' she said, taking a sip of her tea, a little nervously. 'I have been meaning to come past the theatre pub to talk to you about something else.'

'Something more cheerful, hopefully?' he asked.

'I think so.'

He put down his cup and looked so hopeful she felt an awful flip in her stomach as she realised he might have mistaken her meaning. She hated that she was only going to disappoint him again by discussing her career. It was a sore point as he felt that she had chosen it over him when she turned down his proposal of marriage the previous year. That wasn't true; she had turned him down because she had felt that she shouldn't have had to choose. She would never have done that to him had the situation been reversed. 'Um...' She smiled, then toyed with her cup of tea as she admitted, 'well, see, I've started my own amateur dramatics group.'

He frowned, then snorted. 'Of course you have.'

He shook his head, then looked at her in an amused, slightly exasperated way.

'So let me guess, you want to stage something at All the World's a Stage? And hopefully get noticed by someone like George Vaughn?'

She winced. Was she really that transparent?

'Are a lot of people coming to you with this kind of thing now?' she guessed.

He nodded.

'A lot are hopeful of getting spotted but few have had the gumption to start their own amateur dramatics group. You have always been more ambitious than most, though.'

Finley looked away. He sounded slightly bitter. The way he made it sound, her ambition wasn't a good thing.

She bit her lip. She hated that it always came to this between them.

To her surprise, he waved a casual hand. 'I'm not judging,' he said, though of course it did sound like he was. He frowned, then nodded. 'All right. Yes, you can stage a play at the pub.'

She swallowed. 'Really?'

His hazel eyes softened. 'Finley, we might have fought about your career, because I hated that you chose it over me, but I never thought you weren't any *good* – you've always been brilliant, and if it means this much to you I'm happy to help.'

She stared at him. If he thought that, why did he feel so strongly that she should give it up? Shouldn't he want her to do well? Sometimes she felt so frustrated by him. By the barriers he'd forced between them that to her mind could so easily have been overcome. She suspected he felt the same about her. About her refusal to give in and just be what he wanted her to be – his wife, and nothing more.

She blinked. 'Thanks, Simon.'

He winked at her. 'Though I might have to take this piece here as payment,' he said, cutting off a large piece of the Victoria sponge with his cake fork.

She laughed, relieved.

By the time they were ready to leave, he'd warmed up considerably. She'd told him all about the group, and he'd even given her an idea for what to stage.

'Not something bleak like Chekhov. Shaw maybe, but then you have to make sure everyone's on their toes. Shakespeare is always a crowd-pleaser though – it's more forgiving, particularly for amateurs.'

She grinned at him. 'Shakespeare, it is then.'

Archie Greeves put his mug of tea next to the picture of his wife on his coffee table. The picture followed him around his house most days, so that he could have some company, even though she would probably have rolled her eyes at him and called him soft for doing so, had she still been alive.

Gloria had been the practical one in their relationship. In fact, she'd been the one to show him how to rewire the antique chandelier he'd bought.

'It's why we work, sweetheart,' she used to say often enough. 'You're the dreamer, and I'm the one who makes sure we remember to pay the gas man. I can be too practical some-times, and forget that there's more to life than just responsibili-ties. I'd probably never see a need for things like mock-Venetian chandeliers but then I'd never know how beautiful life can be if you give yourself permission to enjoy the fun things in life. You taught me that.'

It was the secret, he'd often thought, to a good marriage. Genuinely liking the differences in the other. All the things Gloria thought were boring about herself, he genuinely found remarkable. They balanced each other out.

It had been three years since Gloria had died and sometimes the loneliness was unbearable. It was why he'd gone back to work; just so that he could have someone to speak to.

This was something he knew she would be proud of. That and the fact that he had joined the Finley Players.

'I don't want you to turn into one of those grumpy old men, when I'm gone. It's not who you are, don't let your shyness get in the way,' she'd said more than once. And yet, for the first few years, that was what happened. It was a gradual loss of the self. Like the fading of a photograph exposed to too much light, he slowly began to lose his customary *joie de vivre*. Without Gloria to push him or to argue with him, he stopped doing the things he loved like visiting antique stores or going to the theatre or cinema, and he found excuses not to visit his nephews and nieces. Their happiness sometimes felt like a mirror to his own loneliness and sadness.

He didn't know how he'd become this beige version of himself.

The news lately was full of the whispers of war. Hitler's ties with Japan, Britain's biggest threat in the Far East, and continuing support from Italy, were seen by many as the drawing up of battle lines.

The thought of another war lit something unexpected within Archie. If they had to go through another one, he didn't want to waste his life any more. He knew better than most how quickly life could be dashed out and he had been guilty of taking the time he had left for granted. When he had been at Woolworths and had seen a bright red and green scarf, he was about to put it back in favour of something less eye-catching, but then he'd stopped and wondered when he had allowed that to happen to himself. When had he started saying yes to so much ordinary?

Later he saw the advertisement for the Finley Players pinned up in his library and it had brought to mind a part of himself he had thought long forgotten – his years in the Cambridge Drama Club, where he admittedly had done more writing of plays and painting of sets than actual acting, but he'd been happy. Then before he could tell himself his usual no, he'd heard Gloria's voice reminding him not to be a grumpy old man. Followed by his own voice saying that he was tired of wasting his own time.

He was so glad he had listened to that voice.

It was something else to think about.

Ever since Italy had annexed Albania, earlier that month, he'd started having that old nightmare from his time as an ambulance driver in the Great War. He dreamt that he was hurrying back to the makeshift hospital, a truck full of injured soldiers in desperate need of attention, when they hit a landmine. It hadn't ever actually happened. Not to him anyway. But he dreamt about it so often, and felt the panic so newly each time, sometimes he really thought it had.

He looked at the photograph now as he dusted the coffee table. 'You were right, you know? You knew it would happen, I'd become sad and too shy to join things.' He often spoke to her like this – like they were still in the middle of a conversation. 'But at least I'm doing something about that now.'

As he closed the door behind him there was a spring in his step that hadn't been there for years.

Finley had made scones for the first official meeting. They had not turned out well at all. Baking, alas, was not one of her talents.

She was feeling unaccountably nervous. There was even more pressure to succeed because somehow she had managed to pencil them in for their first live performance at All the World's a Stage pub theatre in five months' time. She just had to break the news to the others.

But now, fifteen minutes into the first official meeting of the Finley Players, they had already hit their first snag, and Finley could have cheerfully gone back in time and shaken herself for saying that they would be ready.

'You said last week it might be Chekhov, so I spent all week getting my Russian up to snuff,' complained Sunella. 'You want to hear?'

Anita balked. 'No one wants to hear that.'

Sunella swore in Russian.

'What was that?' demanded Anita.

'Something you didn't want to hear,' replied Sunella with a mischievous grin.

Anita looked irate.

'Well I think *The Winter's Tale* is marvellous,' said Archie, possibly in an effort to break up the sudden tension.

'Thanks,' Finley said, who wasn't just thanking him for liking her suggestion.

She had taken Simon's experienced advice – he had a point; a Shakespeare play was all she could think of that might have half a chance of being pulled off reasonably well by untried actors.

'Sorry I'm late,' came a deep voice from behind, and they turned to see Sebastien. Tall, blue-eyed and serious-faced.

Finley's breath caught in her chest. He really was that handsome. Over the past week, she had half-convinced herself that she had imagined how beautiful he was.

She hadn't. When he turned to look at her, she felt her cheeks colour.

'I was held up at work, rather literally at one point,' he said, then held up a bandaged hand.

Despite his friendly manner, there was a cloud behind his eyes. It was the look of someone who was forcing his joviality, and she couldn't help but frown. His eyes held so much unspoken emotion.

'What happened?' asked Finley, looking at Sebastien's hand.

He gave her a crooked smile, and she couldn't help smiling back. Sebastien always seemed slightly serious, so when he shared a lighter side it was unexpectedly disarming, and endearing. Like she could see the shadow of the boy he'd once been, hidden away inside the man.

'I had a disagreement with a printing press,' he said, moving closer to her.

She got a hint of sandalwood and fresh soap. She raised a brow. 'I take it that it won?'

'Hard to say, really. I left it in the corner so it could let off steam.'

She laughed. 'Oh well, poor thing, it was probably under a lot of press-sure.' She emphasised 'press' and they both groaned at her bad pun.

Finley grinned. 'Well, I'm sure once it's cooled down tomorrow you will be friends again.'

He laughed and the way he looked at her made her stomach flutter. She felt her cheeks flood with colour again and bit back a smile, feeling oddly nervous. Being around him made her feel like she was a schoolgirl again. She couldn't remember the last time anyone had made her feel quite like this.

'Who bandaged that for you?' demanded Sunella, making Finley take a reluctant step back as she reached over and snatched up Sebastien's hand. The older woman was staring at it from her five-foot-two stance with a very perplexed expression, oblivious to the way the air was charged around Finley and Sebastien. 'It looks like it was done by someone drunk.'

'Me,' admitted Sebastien, darting an amused look at Finley. 'I wasn't drinking though.'

'Mhmm,' Sunella muttered, not convinced. 'Wait here,' she commanded, holding a slim finger up, then disappeared out of the shop.

They all stared after her fast-retreating sari.

'Well, anyway, I've chosen the play,' said Finley for Sebastien's benefit in the wake of Sunella's sudden departure. 'It's *The Winter's Tale*.'

'Another Shakespeare?' said Sebastien in some surprise.

Finley gave a mock sigh, then grinned. 'Not you too – I've been getting it from all the others.'

Sebastien shook his head. 'I wasn't objecting. I love Shakespeare. He's my mother's favourite playwright, so it always makes me think of her. We used to love going to see one of his plays at the theatre.' He shook his head. 'Before – well—' He stopped himself, as if he were revealing too much.

In the silence, everything that Finley had been reading about Germany and how the Jews were being treated seemed to stretch to fill the space between them. She longed to ask him more about what his life there had been like, how he'd come to be here, all of it, but it just didn't seem like the right moment.

'I can only imagine,' she said instead, realising as she spoke she probably couldn't imagine at all. They stared at each other a little uncomfortably. The easy banter of before had evaporated. Sebastien blinked, looking away; it was as if he'd shared something he hadn't meant to, and his face changed too. Like a wall was coming down suddenly between them. The shadow of the mischievous boy she'd spied within retreating, replaced once more by the all-too-serious man. She didn't like how quickly it disappeared. She stepped closer, and touched his arm.

He looked up in surprise and their gazes held.

Finley said softly, 'Well, I'm glad someone likes my choice, at least.'

'Very much,' he said, staring into her eyes.

They must have been looking at each other for perhaps a beat too long because Archie had to clear his throat to get their attention. Finley blushed to the roots of her hair. Turning away from them all, she surreptitiously swiped at her cheeks, admonishing herself to get a hold of herself. Luckily, she was saved from further embarrassment by the bustling reappearance of Sunella, who was carrying what looked like a dusty old medical bag from before even the Great War.

'Hold out your hand,' she instructed Sebastien.

Sebastien gave Finley a slightly apprehensive look, but did as commanded, and Sunella began taking off his hastily wrapped bandage with cold efficiency, tutting all the while at the hash job he'd done. 'This wasn't even that clean, you silly boy, you could have got an infection. But don't worry, this should help with that,' she said opening up a brown bottle. 'This might sting,' she warned as she applied it liberally to the wound.

Sebastien bit back a curse, wincing, then breathing out a sigh of relief as she re-dressed it with a fresh new bandage. 'Watch what I'm doing here,' she commanded, snapping her fingers in his face. He had been looking over at Finley. 'See how I put this corner here, and tuck this here? Right, all done. How does that feel?'

Sebastien wiggled his fingers. 'Better,' he admitted. 'I can actually move it now. Thanks.'

She shrugged. 'It was a good excuse to dust this off. Been a while,' she admitted.

Finley and Sebastien shared a grin.

The read-through didn't go particularly well.

The play demanded a rather large cast and so Finley had assigned each person numerous roles, and they kept forgetting who they were.

Anita appeared to want to direct as well as act. Archie's nerves seemed to keep getting the better of him too. 'I'm so rusty, sorry – it's just so long since I last acted.'

'It's fine, it's like riding a bicycle, it'll come back to you,' said Finley, really hoping that was true. The old man seemed to have all the inclination but he was so stiff it was a bit painful to watch. If it was possible, he'd actually got *worse*. She had thought of a few exercises for him to try, though, and she was going to pull him aside later to share them with him.

But it wasn't strictly his fault that his performance had deteriorated even further. Anita wasn't making things any easier for him. She had decided perhaps that the best way to tackle his shyness was to show as much attention to it as possible. This worked about as well as one might have expected.

As he stuttered over another line, Anita barked, 'Come now, Archie, just speak up!'

Archie turned a violent shade of red and seemed to be having some trouble with getting his tongue to form the words.

Anita tutted impatiently. 'Just focus your mind.'

Finley felt her hackles rise. She couldn't abide bullies. 'Anita,' she admonished, becoming unexpectedly sharp. 'If someone needs directing, it will come from me, are we clear?'

Anita blinked, looking a bit shocked at being reprimanded. 'I was only trying to help.'

Finley took a deep breath.

Sunella made a 'pfft' sound.

Anita rounded on her. 'What is that supposed to mean?'

'It means that is a funny way to try and help someone, by making things worse.'

'Worse? But I...' she tailed off, noticing Archie flag. To their horror, his eyes shimmered with tears.

'I-I'm sorry, maybe joining this group was a mistake. I thought I was r-ready,' he said, 'since my wife, Gloria, passed I haven't really had the c-courage to get out and do things for some time and um' – he swallowed – 'I thought maybe this would be good for me, but maybe not.' He looked mortified at himself.

Anita looked frozen, her face a rictus of shame and regret.

'Archie,' breathed Finley, unsure of what to say.

'Archie, please don't leave because of me. I-I'll go,' said Anita.

'*No.*'

It was Sebastien who had spoken.

They all turned to look at him in surprise. His tone was forceful, his face serious.

'I think you showed courage, Archie, don't let that go now.'

Archie hesitated. 'I don't feel courageous. I feel like a f-fraud,' he said softly.

Sebastien took a deep breath. He bit his lip. 'We all feel that way sometimes. Maybe as we get older we start becoming a bit more cautious. Myself included. My sister, Katrin, is only twelve and she is fearless.'

'Your sister?' asked Finley.

He nodded. A riot of emotions stormed across his face. Anger, pride and love. He held up his hand. 'That's how I really got this,' he admitted. 'I was distracted at work because I received a letter from my mother telling me that my sister went to the cinema.'

He stared at their blank looks, then gave a short, humourless laugh. 'Exactly. You wouldn't think that would be the height of courage – but in Nazi Germany, it isn't just certain professions that are illegal, or owning property, or travelling on public trans-port unless as a third-class citizen, you also aren't allowed to visit bars or cinemas. Like *dogs*.'

Finley wasn't the only one to gasp. They knew things were

awful, but it wasn't until you heard the details that you realised just how barbaric it truly was.

'She was caught, by a family friend who wanted to give her a fright and reported her to the cinema manager so that she would think twice about going again,' he continued, smiling without humour. 'You know what she told my mother?'

They shook their heads.

'That she'd go back next week – because the day she started believing that she didn't belong was far more frightening than the idea of having to confront the police.'

'Bloody hell,' swore Finley.

Sebastien nodded. 'I think that terrified my parents more than anything else.'

'I can imagine,' said Sunella, clasping her chest.

Archie blinked at Sebastien. 'You must think me an old fool, when that's the sort of hardships your family is facing.'

Sebastien shook his head. 'No, honestly, not at all, I didn't know if I'd come here tonight,' he admitted, turning to Archie. 'I wasn't really meant to join this group, I sort of stumbled in here by mistake last week,' he admitted. 'I've always loved the theatre, and a long time ago I'd hoped that one day I might write a play, but after everything that had happened in Germany, a big part of me thought that this was a part of my life that belonged in the past, like it would be silly to think of joining a group like this, of having fun again, in a way.'

'Oh no son, I'm sorry to hear that,' said Archie.

Sebastien nodded. 'Well, after I heard what happened to my sister, all of that was running through my head again, the idea that I was wasting my time when I should be doing something more active to fight the Nazis – joining the army or writing political articles – and I still want to do that... but well,' he took a deep breath, and admitted, 'I also wanted to come back here and be a part of something, well, fun. I don't think

I've allowed myself to feel that I deserved that for a very long time,' he finished.

The other, biggest reason was the feeling of bone-loneliness he was carrying with him, like a heavy burden, and the pretty girl with the kindest eyes he had seen in the longest time, who had made him feel for a moment less lonely than he'd felt in months, and he couldn't not see her again.

'I knew that if I didn't come, in some way Katrin was right. That I would be giving up something else to the Nazis.' His lips formed into a self-conscious half smile. 'I couldn't help thinking that if she were in my place, she'd come, you know? And that's one of the main reasons I did, and also, probably why I'm telling you about it now,' he admitted.

'I'm glad,' said Archie, who looked very moved by the younger man's words.

'Katrin sounds wonderful,' said Finley, coming closer to touch his arm.

Sebastien looked away for a moment, picturing her freckles, bright eyes and irrepressible smile. 'She is.'

Sebastien bit his lip for a moment as if he were making up his mind about something. Then he looked at Archie and the others. 'There's a poem that helps me get through tough times. My stepfather Gunther gave it to me shortly after the Nazis came into power. I must have read it every week that I lived there, especially when I was working at the newspaper with false papers, because it was illegal to work as a Jew and write for a newspaper, and every evening when I went to work, I used to say it.' He said now. 'I still start my morning every day saying it.'

He took a folded-up piece of paper from his inside his jacket pocket. 'It is "Invictus", by William Ernest Henley.' He looked at Finley. 'I know you're the director,' he said, with a small smile, 'but what if we each did a verse – maybe it will help us all find our inner Katrin?'

Finley felt tears smart in her eyes. Her throat constricted and she nodded. 'I think that would be wonderful.'

Finley began with the first verse, and then pointed at each group member to take the next.

> *Out of the night that covers me,*
> *Black as the pit from pole to pole,*
> *I thank whatever gods may be for my unconquer-*
>   *able soul.*
> *In the fell clutch of circumstance*
> *I have not winced nor cried aloud.*
> *Under the bludgeonings of chance*
> *My head is bloody, but unbowed.*
> *Beyond this place of wrath and tears*
> *Looms but the Horror of the shade,*
> *And yet the menace of the years*
> *Finds and shall find me unafraid.*
> *It matters not how strait the gate,*
> *How charged with punishments the scroll,*
> *I am the master of my fate,*
> *I am the captain of my soul.*

By the end of the poem, there was a shift. The air was charged. They could all feel it.

'I think we should do that every week,' said Archie, who looked quite moved.

'Only if you stay,' said Anita, who looked on the verge of tears herself. She looked like she was fighting some deep emotion within too. Perhaps it was her way of apologising.

Archie swallowed, then nodded. 'Thank you,' he said, but he wasn't just looking at her, it was at all of them.

9

LONDON, JUNE 1939

It was the second week of June when Sebastien was woken by the sound of someone hammering on his bedroom door.

He crept out of bed and stubbed his toe on the chair near the door.

'What is it?' he asked, opening the door with a grimace, not quite ready to greet his landlady at this hour with a smile.

'Phone call,' said Mrs Bower, who looked annoyed. 'I take it that it's serious if they're calling at four in the morning.'

It wasn't a question, more a veiled threat.

Sebastien's throat turned suddenly dry. It could only be news of his family.

His legs were like jelly as he picked up the phone, turning his back on Mrs Bower, who it was clear wasn't about to give him any privacy; perhaps she felt she had a right, considering she had been woken up. He hoped she didn't understand German.

'Mama?' he said, realising that he was holding his breath.

'Sebastien?'

He felt relief flood him as he heard her voice. 'I'm here. What is it? Are you all right?'

'Oh, Sebastien, not really.'

He felt his stomach drop.

'What's happened?'

'Some Nazi hoodlums attacked Gunther on the street for nothing. He was simply walking past them. He's at the Jewish hospital now, recovering. We were turned away by all the hospitals near us, and had to take the train all the way to Cologne. It's so short-staffed, we had to wait hours for him to be seen to, but they have been very kind, and helpful, despite how overworked they are. His doctor says that he's going to make it, but, well, he's in pretty bad shape.'

Sebastien saw spots swarm before his eyes. His stepfather was the only father he'd ever known, and one of the kindest, gentlest people he knew. 'Oh Mama,' he whispered in horror.

She made a funny sound. 'I mean, what do they want from us – we're trying to get out, *they* want us gone too – but they haven't made it easy! We had to sell off our assets and register what we have for the Nazis, so it's not like we have any money in the banks, which would make our application so much easier. We aren't allowed to travel as our passports have been invalidated, so to get out we need special visas, and every day you hear of people being sent to the camps. They've just stopped pretending that they're not trying to destroy us now.'

Sebastien closed his eyes. 'Oh Mama, I don't know what to say.'

'There's nothing to say, Sebastien, we should have followed you, taken you up on your offer to smuggle us out when you left last year. Tried our luck on those false papers.'

He thought so too. But he didn't say it. He didn't want to add to her pain. He wanted to take it away.

'Mama, don't give up, I'm going to the Home Office tomorrow. I've been saving – maybe there is something that can be done to speed this up. I will find out, first thing in the morning.'

'Oh Sebastien, I'm sorry to put this on you, darling, but thank you.'

When he hung up, he sat in the dark for a long time.

Sebastien was at the Home Office. It was stifling hot in the waiting room, and when at last his ticket was called, a man with red hair, freckles and kind brown eyes, who introduced himself as Fred Keith, invited him to take a seat.

'Thank you,' said Sebastien, handing over a file. 'It's all my financials – I have been saving. I'd like to sponsor my family. My mother, sister and stepfather.'

Mr Keith put on his glasses, then looked over the application on his desk, then opened the file Sebastien had given him with his bank records.

'Ah, I see.' He had a faint Scottish accent. 'I'm afraid, Mr Raphael,' he went on, 'it would be rather tricky for you to sponsor your family as per the government's current requirements. See, without your own home they wouldn't let you take on so many people.'

Sebastien sighed, fighting the urge to scream in frustration. He knew he had to remain calm and get this man on his side. 'But if I used my savings to rent my own home, I'd have to pay a deposit and that would mean I wouldn't have enough money to sponsor their visas.'

Mr Keith nodded. 'It's a double-edged sword, I know, Mr Raphael. Perhaps in a few months, once you're able to save up some more, you could come back – so long as you have a place.'

Seeing Sebastien's face fall, Mr Keith bit his lip. 'I have a number for a charity who might be able to help, though I warn you they are pretty swamped too, and from what I hear the people who are getting priority are orphans or families of those who have been sent to concentration camps.

'However, in the meantime there has been real progress on getting some of the children out since last year. A number of organisations have been arranging a transport to collect them, so long as there is someone to sponsor them and take care of them – I think with everything you have here, you might be able to sponsor your sister at the very least, as there's a good chance we might be able to get her on that,' he said. 'As long as she could stay with you.'

Sebastien blinked back tears. It was something. Some progress at last. But still, he didn't want them to be split up.

'I know,' said Mr Keith, who seemed to be reading his thoughts. 'It's unthinkable to split up families. But it might be one of the few options we have.'

Sebastien nodded. 'I'll speak to my family.'

Sebastien wasn't giving up without a fight though. He had to do something to keep them all together. He hated the idea of ripping Katrin away from their parents and it wasn't something he wanted to do if there was another option to be found. His mother and father were going through so much already; it was hard enough being separated from Sebastien – how would they feel having both their children away from them? There had to be another way.

He spent the next few days speaking to Jewish charities, hoping that some of them might be able to help with his family's visas or accommodation so that he could sponsor them, but everyone was so stretched.

He felt tired and hollowed out.

That evening Mrs Bower had dinner guests, including the woman from Mrs Bower's sewing group who had propositioned him, Rita Fitzgerald. She had pale skin and a voluptuous figure that she knew how to accentuate.

'Sebastien. So good to see you. I hope you're staying tonight.

It feels like we never get to see you,' she said, giving him a wide, red-lipstick smile when she saw him coming down the stairs. She was staring up at him, with those enormous green eyes. She was glamorous, but there was an edge to the way she looked at him.

He blinked, taking an involuntary step backwards.

'I brought a bottle of wine.'

'Oh, erm, thank you but—'

'I'm sure things have been difficult and you could use a night off from your worries. Lucy was telling me that your family are stuck in Berlin, and being Jewish things have got so difficult. I want you to know that I am a good listener, if you need to talk...'

Sebastien frowned. He knew she might mean well, but he just didn't have the energy for this now. 'Thank you, that's kind. But I have an appointment.'

'Perhaps another time?'

He gave her a small smile. 'Perhaps.'

Sebastien reluctantly made his way down the street on wooden legs. He was walking past the Thrifty Thimble, half-wishing it was a Thursday night as he could do with a distraction, and contemplating getting himself something to eat at a café, or even a beer, when a pair of warm brown eyes and the sort of smile that seemed like the sun after the longest night stopped him in the street.

It was Finley, locking up.

'Sebastien?'

'Hi,' he said, smiling. 'I was just thinking of you.'

Her eyes widened. 'Me?'

He blushed. 'I mean, the group. I've had a bit of a day, and I wished it was a Thursday – could do with some distraction.'

'Oh, I'm sorry to hear that you've had a tough day.'

'Thanks.'

'You know, I was actually on my way to meet Archie for a drink, why don't you join us?'

He blinked. 'Um.'

'"Invictus", remember?' she said with a wink. 'Not sure if that actually means courage or not, but, well, it does to me.'

He gave her a half smile. 'To me too. All right. Thanks.'

He followed after her to a pub round the corner called the Wily Fox. Archie was sitting at a table at the back. Wearing a striking scarlet and black scarf.

'Sebastien,' said the older man. 'Oh, this is a lovely surprise.'

'Found him wandering past the shop and so I marched him over.'

'Good girl!' said Archie, with a twinkle in his eye.

Sebastien smiled. It felt like the first time in a week. It was good to have friends. 'First round is on me, what's everyone having?'

'Thank you, good sir. Sherry for me,' said Archie.

'Red wine, please, medium,' said Finley.

When he came back with their drinks, Finley had removed her coat. He took a seat next to her.

'Finley said you've had a bit of a bad day?' asked Archie.

Sebastien looked at Finley, and raised a brow.

She smiled. 'Sorry, we're just hoping we can help.'

Sebastien blew out his cheeks. He wanted to offload to them, to tell them everything that had happened. But it just felt like so much, too much, in this small cheerful pub.

There was the danger he might actually break down into tears.

So he just said, through a throat thick with emotion, that he grunted to clear, 'It's just family stuff. We're working on the visas, it's just a bit tricky.'

Finley touched his arm. 'I'm sorry.'

'My brother, Milton, works at the Home Office,' said Archie. 'I don't know if he'd actually be able to do anything, but I can try to set up a meeting – maybe there's something?'

Sebastien blinked, then had to stop his chin from wobbling. 'That would be very kind.'

Archie nodded. 'It's the least we can do.'

'Thanks,' he said, and meant it.

10

It was nearing midnight when Sebastien got home. Mrs Bower was asleep in her chair in the kitchen. He was fortunate with Mrs Bower in that she didn't set a curfew, as so many boarding homes did; that just wouldn't work for him, not with his two jobs and his night-time shifts at the factory. As a result, he was the only tenant with a key. This was something of an honour, and he was often reminded of it by Mrs Bower.

Although he had never yet failed to lock the door behind him, he knew that Mrs Bower was paranoid that he might, which was why she sometimes waited up.

He walked quietly past so as not to disturb her, with one thought on his mind: sleep.

He groped for the light switch in his room, and let out an involuntary yell when he saw that there was someone in his bed. Someone naked.

It was Rita Fitzgerald.

'Oh, did I surprise you,' she said, with a slow smile, as she reached for a gold cigarette case, took out a slim cigarette, rather too slowly and casually for his nerves, and lit it. He saw, from some cold part of his brain, that she had probably been there a while; there were two glasses and a bottle of red wine on his nightstand.

'Mrs Fitzgerald—'

She laughed. 'Darling, you absolutely are allowed to call me Rita at this point.'

He frowned. 'Mrs Fitzgerald, please, this isn't what you want – here, cover yourself,' he said, reaching for his robe on the back of the door and throwing it to her.

She made no move to take it. 'Come now, Sebastien,' she said, with a teasing smile. 'You don't have to be coy. You're a grown-up and a beautiful-looking man, with needs. You're allowed to have fun, you know? In fact, I think you deserve it after all your troubles.' She reached for a glass of wine and took a sip. There was ring of bright-pink lipstick on the rim. 'I think we could have a lot of fun.'

He gave her a half smile. For almost a second, he was even tempted. It would be so easy to forget the past week this way; but he knew she was only doing this to get back at her cheating husband.

He frowned, then took a seat next to her. 'I know, but that doesn't mean we should.'

She started to look slightly uncomfortable at last. 'Don't you find me attractive?' Her big green eyes filled with tears, which began to spill over alarmingly. She crossed an arm over her ample breasts. He could see that, behind her bravado, she was really hurting.

The truth was that she was very attractive. Having a naked woman in his bedroom was definitely having an effect on him. He was human, after all. But he didn't think she would feel better for it, and, honestly, it would just make the whole situation with his landlady tricky. He didn't need any more complications. Also, well, there was a small part of him that couldn't help thinking of a girl who fizzed with the kind of internal joy that was hard to resist, and the kind of smile that made him feel like he'd come out of the cold after a long winter.

'It's not that,' he admitted.

'Am I too old? Is it like with my Stanley? He used to be wild for me, you know? All the men were. But I'm in my late thirties now, and so what – that's it? I'm put out to pasture?'

Sebastien really didn't want to have to deal with this, but he had no choice. 'Mrs— Rita, don't be silly, you are very beautiful, I don't doubt they all still go a bit wild, but I don't think it would be right for us. I think you need to speak to your husband, see if you can work it out.'

'But he doesn't want me, and now neither do you!'

He realised with horror that she was more than a little drunk, as she began to cry, rather loudly.

'N-no, please, Rita, please don't cry,' he whispered.

Rita began to howl desperately.

Sebastien jumped off the bed in horror. Oh hell, what was he going to do?

Soon there was the sound of footsteps pounding up the stairs.

This can't be happening, thought Sebastien, putting his hands in his hair in frustration and groaning.

There was an insistent knock at the door.

'Sebastien, do you have a lady friend in there?' demanded Mrs Bower, sounding outraged.

'No, um, it's not that, Mrs Bower.'

Rita's crying continued unabated.

'You do have someone in there, I'm not stupid!' cried Mrs Bower.

'Please, Mrs Bower, it's not what you think—'

'Oh really? It sounds like it's exactly what I think – I'm coming in!' cried his landlady, who sounded furious. 'You know this is utterly against the rules.'

Sebastien turned in horror, realising in his exhaustion that he had failed to lock his bedroom door behind him as he usually did.

He had time to hastily put the robe over most of Rita's nakedness, but Mrs Bower had seen enough. Taking in the miserable state of her drunken friend, the wine glasses and the bottle, she jumped to the only logical conclusion.

'Oh, poor Rita, has he hurt you?'

Sebastien gasped. 'No!'

Thankfully Rita managed to shake her head in the negative. 'N-no, not physically.'

Sebastien shoved his hands into his hair. This was a nightmare. He only wished he were dreaming.

'I see. So you took advantage of her. Fed her wine and then had your way with her? Sebastien, how could you take advantage of her like this – you know how vulnerable she is, after everything with her husband.'

'No, it wasn't like that please, Mrs Bower. I came home to find Rita in my bed.'

He felt a bit bad exposing her to Mrs Bower – he never would have said anything if she would have just left – but he needed somewhere to live.

Mrs Bower's eyes bulged and she stared at Sebastien in utter contempt. 'How dare you put the blame on her – it's one thing to find you two together like this, but to lie about it and diminish Rita's character like that in the process is a despicable display of cowardice, Sebastien.'

Sebastien's mouth fell open in shock. 'No, Mrs Bower, I promise you that isn't what I was doing. I only meant—'

'To cover yourself, no, I understand you perfectly,' said Mrs Bower, coldly. 'I think that under the circumstances it would be best for everyone if you left first thing in the morning. And don't expect a reference.'

Sebastien turned to Rita with imploring eyes, and finally, in her drunken, emotional state, perhaps she began to see the damage she had caused, because she swallowed, then said, 'We were both to blame, Lucy.'

'That is good of you to say, Rita,' said Mrs Bower.

Sebastien pinched the bridge of his nose. Clearly Rita didn't want to admit the truth to her friend, and as a result she'd got him kicked out of his home.

'Come on, Rita, let's get you to the spare room,' said Mrs Bower, helping her friend into Sebastien's robe and then out of the room.

Before she left, Mrs Bower said over her shoulder, 'I think it's best if you leave before anyone gets up, Mr Raphael.'

Sebastien closed his eyes, then nodded. At this point, what else was there to say?

Frank found him asleep on the step outside the printing press. Sebastien felt a gentle prodding between his ribs, and opened a pair of bleary eyes to find the older man standing over him and holding out an old yellow tin mug full of coffee in his thick hands. 'You look like you need this,' Frank said. Sebastien winced as he sat up. Sleeping on the cold concrete had not done his lower back any favours.

'Thanks,' he said, and took the mug gratefully. It warmed his cold hands.

Frank took a seat beside him. 'So, I'm guessing there's another reason you're here this early, one that hasn't got anything to do with how committed you are to your job?'

Sebastien gave him a wry smile, then frowned. With his free hand he pinched the bridge of his nose. Then he began to tell Frank a summarised version of what had happened when he'd got home the previous night, and the misunderstanding he'd had with his landlady.

'Oh no, she stitched you up proper,' said Frank, who then began to chortle.

'It's not funny.'

'It's a little bit funny.'

Sebastien took a sip of coffee, and then gave a short snort. It was a little bit funny.

'Would have been easier to have just slept with her,' said Frank. 'Who knew being a gentleman would cost so much.'

'Tell me about it. No good deed goes unpunished and all that.'

'That your stuff?' said Frank, cocking his head towards the suitcase that had acted as Sebastien's rather hard pillow and pointing out the obvious.

Sebastien nodded.

'Right, well, you can sleep on the sofa at mine till you find somewhere new. Berta won't mind, she's always wanting to get more meat on those bones, you know.'

Sebastien was touched. 'Frank, that's too kind. I mean, you don't have to do that.'

Frank laughed, 'Son, it's not like I'm going to let you sleep out here every night. Can't have that on my conscience. Besides, that's what friends are for.'

Sebastien clamped a hand on the older man's shoulder. 'Thanks.'

'I'll warn you though, my grandchildren are staying with us too, so it's going to be a bit noisy.'

Frank hadn't been joking. It was crowded in the small flat. Two grandchildren under the age of ten, Frank's wife and daughter, and him. Sebastien was only getting in the way.

There weren't any boarding houses that were willing to take him without references, so Frank offered to say that he had been living with him.

It was another reason to feel grateful.

Sebastien knew he probably should have felt angry or

resentful at Mrs Bower and how things had turned out, but in a way it was the push he'd needed to get out of the tiny attic room and uncomfortable home he'd been living in for the past six months.

He was still in a horrible limbo with the Home Office as, while he was tempted to just go and rent his own place, he couldn't because then he wouldn't have the money his family would need for the government to grant their visas.

He was really hoping that Archie's brother might have a solution. Right then, it was his only hope.

That and the fact that Katrin might be getting on one of the Kindertransports. It hadn't been finalised yet, but wherever he went now he would have to ask for a room for his sister too.

The only trouble was that, everywhere he looked, the prices were quite extortionate, and none of the landlords wanted to have someone like Sebastien who would be coming home at all hours of the evening. Not to mention someone who was also looking for a space for their little sister.

It was just at the point when he was about to give up when he saw a notice in a shop window for a room to let not far from the Thrifty Thimble. He telephoned the number and was invited to come and see it that afternoon.

Sebastien was welcomed inside a rather spacious Victorian house by a woman named Isabelle Castle, in her mid- to late fifties, who lived there with her daughter, and her son when he was home from university.

It was tastefully furnished, with lots of beautiful paintings on the walls. On the mantelpiece in the living room, he could see a row of framed photographs, but they were too far away for him to make them out clearly.

He accepted a cup of tea from Mrs Castle.

She was friendly and hadn't said anything about his accent, which all seemed to be a good sign.

'You have two jobs? Is that right?' she asked, looking at him with a curious expression in her grey eyes.

'I'm saving for my own place,' he said.

'And your family – do you have anyone nearby?'

She was clearly astute, and no doubt had gathered he was a refugee.

He shook his head. 'I'm hoping that my family will be able to come over from Germany soon. It's one of the reasons I'm working so much, I plan on sponsoring them.'

Her face showed real compassion. 'That must be hard, I hope they can follow soon.'

He took a deep breath.

He didn't know why but the unexpected kindness caused a lump to form in his throat. She didn't get overly dramatic, just in the nicest way acknowledged that it must have been difficult, and he felt quite touched.

'Thanks.' He swallowed. 'Actually, my circumstances have changed a little in that the Home Office have said that my little sister Katrin might be able to come. She's twelve. Um, they have been arranging transports for some of the children to flee.'

Mrs Castle stared at him, a look of sympathy on her face. 'They're separating them from their families.'

He nodded.

'We haven't got the green light yet but well, if we do, I was hoping for a rental that could take her too, but well, you only have the three rooms.'

She shook her head. 'And the dining room, she would be welcome to use that.'

He blinked up at her. 'Really?'

'Oh yes, I love children, so that would be no bother.'

Sebastien couldn't help the smile that spread across his face. Unlike all the other places where he'd been politely refused over the past week, Isabelle didn't mind that he worked odd hours. 'We're used to that. My daughter often has odd hours too, and uses the key underneath the flower pot outside to let herself in. I can't very well object if you do the same, considering you're saving for such a good cause. You can do the same when you move in. When do you think that will be?'

He was surprised, and pleased that she was offering it to him. 'As soon as possible?'

'Suits me. You can move in tonight, if you like.'

'That would be ideal. I'm staying with my friend, Frank and his family, they're lovely...'

She grinned. 'I'm sensing a but?'

'But it's a bit crowded. My friend has grandchildren, they're seven and nine. I'm considered something of a pet.'

She made an 'O' with her lips as she whistled. Then she laughed. 'No wonder you look so tired.'

He grinned, then nodded. More tired than usual, and that was saying something.

'Well, don't worry, it's pretty quiet here most of the time. Well, unless my daughter is around, she can talk for England, but other than that you should have plenty of peace and quiet.

He felt a flash of sadness as he thought of his own family.

She showed him to what would be his room. It was near the kitchen and was bigger than his old one, and much more comfortably furnished. It had chintz curtains in a blue and white delft pattern, a double bed, with a matching delft-inspired coverlet. And beneath a window was a leather armchair next to a bookcase in the corner. It felt almost palatial compared to what he was used to.

'There's a kettle for you, but you're welcome to use the kitchen any time. Do you like tea or coffee?'

He must have looked at her oddly because she said, 'Germans are usually more coffee drinkers, aren't they?'

'Yes, though my mother lived in England for a while when I was born and she grew fond of tea, so I don't mind either.'

Tea was one of the only things his mother had liked about that time in her life. He didn't mention that part though.

Sebastien was just unpacking his suitcase into his bureau when he heard the front door open and close, followed by the fast tap of heels on the linoleum as someone rushed past in something of a hurry.

'Mummy, can't stay long, just wanted to quickly to pop in and tell you I'll be home late tonight. It's the final push for costumes, so wish me luck.'

Drawn to the sound, he came out of his room, still holding the two jumpers he could claim to his name, only to gasp.

He wasn't the only one.

Finley, who had turned round at the sound of his approach, stared at him with wide eyes.

'Sebastien? What are you doing here?'

'I... well, I've just moved in,' he said, shocked to find her there. And she'd just shouted 'Mummy' up the stairs. How was it possible that Finley was the daughter Isabelle had been referring to?

Hearing the commotion, his new landlady – and, he took it, Finley's mother – came down the stairs at something of a gallop.

'Fin, darling, before you go I just wanted to let you know—oh!' she exclaimed. 'There you are, Mr Raphael. Um, darling, I just wanted to let you know we've got a new lodger, Mr Sebastien Raphael.'

Finley's face was a picture. 'Mum, this is brilliant,' she said, then looked at Sebastien and laughed. 'We know each other already! Sebastien is in my drama group.'

Isabelle frowned. 'What?'

Sebastien nodded.

Isabelle stared at him and then said, 'Oh no, but you seemed so sensible.'

Sebastien thought she might be joking, though he wasn't sure.

Her lips twitched though.

'He is,' said Finley, loyally.

'I didn't put the two together,' said Sebastien, who felt, even though Finley didn't seem to mind the turn of events at all, that *he* needed an explanation. 'Your surnames...?'

Isabelle pulled a face. 'Ah, yes. Well, blame my husband for that,' she said. 'He started calling her Finley, which was his surname – our surname – as soon as it became clear that she didn't quite suit her Christian name, Prudence, well, at all, God bless her.' She laughed, looking at Finley, who just shrugged and then grinned. 'But she is every bit a Finley,' continued Isabelle.

Finley nodded. 'For better or worse. They're mad as hatters apparently.'

'Also stubborn, too confident for their own good, and total dreamers.'

'Yep,' said Finley, winking at him. 'You say all of this like it's a bad thing, Mummy.'

Isabelle rolled her eyes and shot Finley a look of resignation mixed with affection. 'See what I mean?'

He laughed and found himself smiling.

Isabelle continued, as if he'd asked her a question. 'So, yes, I just said Castle – which was my maiden name – in the advert so that it wouldn't be confusing for the new lodger. But Mrs F works too.'

Sebastien nodded, then frowned as he looked at Finley rather seriously. 'I mean, only if it is all right with you, though.'

Finley grinned, widely. 'I don't mind if you call her Mrs F.'

He laughed again, and said, 'No, I mean – if I stay?'

'Sebastien, of course it's all right! I'm really glad it's not a stranger.'

Then she looked at her mother. 'You are a dark horse, I never thought you'd actually get a lodger.'

'Have to keep you on your toes, darling.'

'Well, you succeeded,' said Finley, looking at Sebastien in wonder.

Sebastien hoped that was a good thing.

11

LONDON, JUNE 1939

Archie looked at his photograph of Gloria.

'Gloria, you should see that young man's eyes – they're haunted. Last time I saw eyes like that was during the war. The ones who came back had a similar look. Like they've seen things that can't be unseen.'

Archie had driven an ambulance in the Great War because his chronic asthma had meant he wasn't fit to be in the trenches. He'd got as close as he could to the fighting, and vowed that if he could help he would. He'd saved many lives, risking his own countless times, and, even though he hadn't been the one fighting, it hadn't stopped the nightmares. They'd increased lately, now that it just felt like history was repeating itself.

'Helpless... it was awful to see – after everything he's already been through. He was so kind to me when I had my wobble in the beginning and I thought, well, maybe this is what we could do for him. I'll speak to Milton about it.'

He met his little brother every Tuesday in the shabby café round the corner for a catch- up. It was Milton's way of looking out for him since he'd lost his wife.

Milton, who in his late forties was fifteen years Archie's

junior, and handsome, arrived looking tired, stressed and thin and it was Archie's turn to feel worried for him.

His dark-brown hair, which was usually neatly combed to one side, was sticking up slightly, and there were dark rings beneath his wide hazel eyes. He was also smoking too much, which was always a sign that he was anxious.

Milton sighed as he took a bite of his toast, then began to speak about his work in such a defeated way that Archie's heart plummeted to his shoes. 'You wouldn't believe, Arch, how many people are trying to get across the border now. Charities are putting on pressure. I mean the only real successes are getting some of the children across, though it's a sorry business splitting up families. I'm getting calls daily from acquaintances asking for me to pull strings. I'm at my wits' end. Unofficially there's very little I can do – we have opened up our immigration quotas under the present circumstances but there's already a backlash in place.'

'But why though? I mean, it's not like anyone can pretend not to know what Hitler wants to do to the Jews now – they've come out and said it – they want them gone.'

Milton rubbed his forehead. 'I know. The public is very sympathetic to that by and large. But you know how it is, some people can't think of something awful over there as being anything to do with them.

'Then there's always that small, but vocal sector of the populace who're afraid we'll be overrun with foreigners. Even though by percentages we haven't actually let that many in. But the press doesn't help – they have run with that line often enough and have spread this idea that we will be overflowing. Then there's the undeniable fact that the economy is at a low point, jobs are scarce; there's fear that the refugees will take their work. I mean, it's not true – many refugees are skilled, and they're bringing that here, and as they put their skills and money back it helps the economy to grow, and a lot of the refugees are willing to do the work we don't go in for... but the perception persists that they're a drain.'

It seemed like a well-worn lecture, one he gave a lot, and Archie felt a stab of empathy. It must be so frustrating.

'But if you know that, can't you tell the papers – explain things?'

There had been a lot of articles about the threat of a foreign invasion of refugees over the past few years. That had swung considerably over the last year, in favour of refugees coming in, particularly with the events of Kristallnacht, but it wasn't like those fears just went away. Perhaps, he thought, it needed addressing more officially.

'Yes, well, how can we when many of the ministers in the government feel that way themselves? So many people become blind when they only listen to their fear.'

'That's tough, Milton, I'm sorry. It's also awful timing of me because I'm afraid that I'm going to be one of those horrid people who ask for your help with a family visa too.'

'Oh Archie,' complained Milton, pausing between bites of baked beans. 'Not you too. I can't just magic up a visa, there's a process.'

'I know, but there's a friend who needs my help. He's already applied on behalf of his family. But it's tricky. He hasn't given me all the details but, well, he told me how his stepfather was beaten up and they're desperate to get out of Germany in case they're sent to one of those awful camps they've built.'

The stories of these places were enough to give anyone nightmares. Later, they would find out that they were even worse than anything they might have ever imagined, but the idea of forced labour camps, sterile concrete facilities and freezing cold winters seemed horrific enough.

Milton frowned. 'Bloody awful business.' Then he took out a notebook. 'What's his name?'

'Sebastien Raphael.'

Milton nodded.

'I don't know how long these things take but I was hoping maybe with your help...'

'It might go faster? If only I had that kind of power.'

'I know.'

If anyone could have used it for good it would be his little brother.

'Well, let me try to get a spot in the diary and see if I can be of any help.'

'That's all anyone can ask.'

Milton shook his head as he finished the last of his stone-cold breakfast. 'You'd be surprised.' Then he shrugged. 'Not that you can blame them.'

'No,' agreed Archie. 'You really can't. I just hope that things get better. I mean surely Germany will have to come right, they can't carry on like this for ever. I just feel for the ordinary Germans who have been forced to go along with this. I hope they can be delivered of those Nazis.'

Milton sighed. 'I feel like it might just get a lot worse before they are able to expel them.'

'I hope you're wrong.'

Milton nodded. 'Yes, so do I.'

After their breakfast, Archie watched his younger brother walking away, and something about his stance, as he put on his grey hat and coat and made his way out onto the rain-lashed streets of London, reminded him of Atlas, bearing the weight of the world on his shoulders.

12

LONDON, JUNE 1939

It had been a week since Sebastien had moved into Finley's house.

In that time she'd only really crossed paths with him twice, and once was a midnight trip to the loo, which had been a bit awkward, and also a bit thrilling.

Seeing him in just a plain white t-shirt with pyjama bottoms and bare feet had felt incredibly intimate, that late at night, and they'd shared a bashful goodnight in passing.

This morning was the first time she'd ever really seen him for longer than a few minutes.

She didn't see him sitting at the kitchen table when she entered, yawning, her hair in curlers and wearing a very old pink robe.

'Morning,' he said, and she nearly jumped out of her skin.

'Morning,' she replied, biting her cheek to suppress the wide smile that was spreading across her face at the thought that his was a rather nice face to greet first thing.

Finley realised she was staring at him, so she looked away, forgetting why she'd come to the kitchen in the first place.

'Would you like a cup of tea?' he offered as he made his way to the kettle. His lips twitched in amusement. 'Your mother has given me instructions on how to make it.'

Finley chortled. 'I can well imagine that. Tea would be lovely, thank you.'

As he made his way to the kettle, she saw that his pyjamas bottoms were too short and the sight was oddly endearing.

It was too early in the day for this, she thought.

She took a seat at the scarred wooden table next to where Sebastien had been sitting, and saw that he had been writing in a notebook. The page that was open was covered in indecipherable black ink. As she squinted at it, she saw heard a noise, then blushed when she realised she'd been caught staring at his notebook.

He bit his lip. 'It's my first article in English.'

Her eyes widened. 'Really?'

He nodded. 'It's not easy writing in a second language, I've had to keep my word choices simple and my sentences short.'

He frowned.

'I don't know if any newspapers would be interested in what I have to say but there's a release in just getting some of it out,' he said, placing the brown teapot on the scarred wooden table and then setting out two porcelain cups.

'I can't imagine what it must have been like.'

He looked at her. 'It's hard for me to comprehend, and I lived it, you know? For the last decade, it was just this slow, growing hatred towards the Jews, and it sounds crazy that you can almost get used to it, but in a way our family did. We kept doing these little adjustments, you know? Hoping things would be a bit better as a result, and for a while things were.

'Then the Nuremberg Laws came into effect in '35 and Jews were declared second-class citizens; it became illegal for us to marry Aryans – the Germans of pure blood – and then somehow, we got used to that, and for the next two years it seemed like, well, this is as bad as it might get.

'Then suddenly we weren't allowed to own property, and I had to give up my flat, and rent in a Jewish neighbourhood.'

He looked away.

Finley could imagine how hard it must have been to have gone from being a political journalist, with a glittering career ahead of him, to watching it all crumble to dust, in the space of a few months.

'Soon, I wasn't allowed to write any more. My boss, Samuel —' his voice trembled and she could hear the emotion behind his words, 'didn't want to accept it either, and so I had a friend who I went to college with forge some papers so that I could work under an alias, but I had to work at night when no one was around, and on very reduced pay. In the end someone informed on us though, and that's why I had to flee Berlin. It took Samuel months to get his name cleared, and that was only because his sister is married to a Nazi. Since then, well, people like me have been stripped of their citizenship – I mean you no longer have a country – it's terrifying and just makes my blood boil, I just want to be able to do something about it.'

Finley shook her head, feeling a bubbling of anger within her. 'It makes me angry, this inexplicable hatred, I can't under-stand why any of the normal Germans are going along with it.'

'I don't know that they all do. I mean, it's not like here, it's not a democracy in Germany. The Nazi Party is like the world's deadliest cult – any word spoken against them is treated as trea-son, and it can cost you your life. It's not safe to voice any opinion against them.'

Finley looked shocked. 'You almost sound sympathetic.'

'I'm not, but I do understand, in a way, how the Germans have found themselves forced into this. I wish it wasn't but Germany is still the place I consider home, and I find it sad that it couldn't shake itself of the Nazis. I can get to some degree why the party became so powerful – I mean for so many they see Hitler as a saviour, restoring their national pride. They've also used the Jews as a bit of convenient scapegoat for so many of the country's problems – from poverty to unemployment and inflation – they have these books on how to recognise a Jew, and they're all these horrid stereotypes of greedy moneylenders and such.'

Finley gasped. 'That's just so awful.'

He sighed. 'It feels good to get a normal reaction to that.'

'I think the fact that you wouldn't be shocked by it shocks me most of all. Does writing help?'

He stared at her. 'Yes, I think so. Makes me feel like I do have a voice.'

'I'd love to read your article when you're done.'

He bit his lip, then laughed nervously. 'You know, I've never been nervous to share my stories before, but they were never personal before – they were things I believe in, things I reported on, but never written from my own experiences, and it's... different.'

It was raw, and exposing, but it felt good to get it out.

Finley's eyes were warm. 'You don't have to share it if you don't want to.'

He smiled at her. 'I can be brave.'

'I think you're already the bravest person I know.'

They looked at each other for a long moment, and Finley blushed. 'Another cup of tea?'

'Why not?'

As she handed him a cup, he offered her the sugar bowl. 'Sugar?'

'Three please.'

He looked taken aback and she laughed. 'I know. My mother always insists on no sugar for me whenever she's around, so I have to get my fun when I can.'

He grinned.

She took a sip, and then sighed in satisfaction. 'Bliss.'

'In that case I'll go wild myself,' he said, and added a lump to his own.

'Steady on,' she said.

'I'll just tell her you're a bad influence.'

They shared a grin.

'She will find that very easy to believe.'

He laughed.

Finley was surprised at how easy it was to speak with him; she hadn't expected it to feel so natural. She'd been happy when she found out that Sebastien was to be their new lodger. Perhaps a little excited at the thought of seeing his handsome face more often, which would certainly brighten her days. But she had worried that it could also be a little awkward. So far, apart from passing each other in the middle of the night, it really hadn't.

13

LONDON, JUNE 1939

Katrin was coming to England.

The man from the Home Office, Fred Keith, had been as good as his word and now Sebastien had received the letter to say that his sister had a place as early as next week on the Kindertransport, the system that the government had put in place to rescue thousands of Jewish children, giving them temporary visas, in the hopes that one day they would be able to go home and return to their families.

His mother was tearful but happy when he'd phoned to tell her the news.

'It's for the best, my darling,' she'd said. 'Gunther is still recovering in the Jewish hospital, but hopefully we will all be able to join you soon.'

Sebastien felt once again that surge of hatred towards the Nazi thugs who had beaten up his stepfather for no other reason than that he was Jewish.

'I hope so,' he said, and told her about Archie's brother Milton. Who he'd gone to see the day before, who'd said he would look at what other avenues might be available. It had been a brief meeting, but Sebastien had liked the man, and, though it was dangerous to get his hopes up, nonetheless he was feeling more positive as a result.

It seemed awful to think of splitting them up, but getting Katrin out would be a step in the right direction.

'Mama, I wish it was all of you. I hate that it's taking so long.'

'I do too my darling, but it takes as long as it takes. Besides, as crazy as it sounds, knowing Katrin will be safe with you – well, that's one good thing, the first good thing. If all goes well, perhaps we'll all be together by the end of the year. Maybe even celebrate Hanukkah.'

Sebastien closed his eyes as he held the telephone to his ear. 'Mama, that sounds wonderful.'

When he told Isabelle and Finley the news, they were almost as excited as he was. He offered though to start looking for a new place soon. 'I know you said it would be fine, but I don't want to get in your way, and having a child around is an adjustment,' he said.

'One I am very accustomed to, I can assure you, as I had to raise two by myself after we lost my husband in the war. Besides, it will be wonderful to have someone young about the place,' countered Isabelle.

Finley nodded. 'My mother needs someone to fuss over, Sebastien, your sister would be doing me a favour,' she joked.

He grinned, and she turned serious. 'Besides, you're saving every penny so you can sponsor your family – you can't go and rent a place a place and throw all your money away! We'd love to have her. We can turn the dining room into a bedroom, isn't that right Mummy?' who nodded.

'Exactly,' said her mother, who was looking at Finley approvingly. 'It's better to be sensible about things.'

'Are you sure?'

'Of course!' said Finley. 'I can't wait to meet her.'

'It will be lovely,' agreed Isabelle. 'Like I said, it will be wonderful to have a child around.' She grinned. 'I *do* like having someone to fuss over,' she admitted. 'Also, it gives me an excellent excuse to learn German.'

They both turned to her in surprise.

'Well, you said that Katrin doesn't speak English, she didn't learn it in school like you did, Sebastien.'

He shook his head. 'She was taught it but she didn't really apply herself, and that's what she needs to do now,' he said sternly.

Isabelle frowned. 'Yes, you're probably right, but also, she's been through enough and had to let go of so much, I don't want to be one of those people who try to take that part of her away too.'

14

LONDON, JULY 1939

It was a beautiful summer day in July when the ship docked in Harwich. Outside, the East Anglian sun was mild and the flat, golden green countryside made way for big wide-open skies.

Sebastien waited on the gangplank for his little sister to arrive, with his heart in his mouth. He was so anxious he felt sick to his stomach and hadn't been able to sleep. What if she wasn't on the ship? He'd been assured that she was, but still, what if something had happened? Some of the stories he'd heard of people being sent to camps made him break out into a cold sweat.

He looked at every little face as it passed him by for signs of his sister.

It was Katrin who found him. Her small voice like a bell, coming from a few metres away. 'Sebastien! Sebastien!'

He turned and saw her smiling widely at him, with her familiar bobbed brown hair and fringe, above very blue eyes. Her hair so different from all the other young girls, their regulation plaits and pigtails and heavily scraped-back hair. His mother had been a hairdresser, and she didn't hold any truck with styles that didn't suit someone.

He began to run and she jumped into his arms, and dangled there, feet off the ground, for at least a full minute. Until she started to complain, 'You're crushing me.' But she was laughing as she said it.

He let her down, but didn't let her go.

She seemed so much older, but still so tiny and fragile with her heart-shaped face and large blue eyes, so like his.

'I thought you'd be fatter,' she said.

He laughed, then took the small brown suitcase she was holding, and draped his arm round her.

For the first time in a year he felt almost right.

'Mama said to tell you not to do that,' she said, as his face seemed to drop. 'Don't scrunch, don't be sad,' she said, lifting a hand and pressing between the frown lines on his face. 'She said we'll all be together again soon, so you mustn't be sad.' She appeared to be fighting the tears herself as her chin wobbled. He realised that she was trying desperately to put on a brave face.

Once again, he would learn courage from her.

He gave her another bone-crushing side hug. 'Well, if she said that, then you know it's true.'

'Yes,' she said simply, through a throat that sounded thick with emotion. 'Mama always gets her way, you know that,' she grinned. She was trying to make light.

They made their way past the rest of the new arrivals, many of whom weren't as fortunate as Katrin, and didn't have a loving family member there to greet them but a stranger who had sponsored them, a stranger who was now responsible for them.

She told him about the long journey and the kind people who came to help them. 'They were wonderful, there was one lady who couldn't speak any German, but she was nice and she was trying her best. She had these funny little cakes she had made especially, sconces, I think they're called, you have them with jam and she even said at home she serves them with cream

– it was delicious. I was with her part of the way here, and she taught me some English words.'

'Oh right, such as?'

'More cake, please?'

He laughed aloud. 'Essential.'

'I thought so,' she said rather seriously. Then she looked at him, and said, 'So, tell me about your girlfriend?'

He gave her a wide-eyed look, 'I don't have a girlfriend.'

'Really – the one from the drama group you now live with, she's not your girlfriend?'

'How did you hear about that?'

'You told Mama, she told me.'

'Well, she's just a friend, that's all.'

Katrin frowned. 'I owe Papa money now. I said she was.'

'Well, you'll just have to pay him when they get here,' said Sebastien, tousling her hair.

They stared at each other, hoping that would be true, then she pulled back: 'Hey, hey, not the hair.'

Katrin was, it must be said, every bit as fastidious as his mother about her coiffure, and she had told him in a letter that one of the things she was most looking forward to about living in London was trying out one of the new hairstyles, not to mention being allowed to visit the cinema and theatres again – all things that she hadn't been allowed to do back home. He was glad that she was treating it this way, and that she was so upbeat about it. Though, behind her sunny smile, he could see that she was putting on a brave face. He was doing the same; it seemed inconceivable that she was here and their parents weren't. His heart ached for them, even as it lifted at the sight of his sister's face.

'I'm surprised she wasn't here, your non-girlfriend.'

He looked at Katrin, and grinned. 'You are going to love her.'

'Oh, I know that already,' she said. 'Mama read the bits

about her to us in your letters and she seems so funny, and feisty, not like the girls back home.'

'She's not like anyone,' he agreed. 'Finley and her mother, Isabelle, wanted to come too, but I thought it would be better if it was just us two for a little while,' he explained.

She smiled. 'That sounds good too.'

The journey back to London took a few hours by train, and it was afternoon by the time they got the Tube into Notting Hill. As they walked, Katrin stared at all the houses. 'They're so charming. I thought they would be like the ones in the cities back home, like say Berlin. Are there any parks or lakes nearby?'

'Yes, a bit further out – we can go to one today if you like, if you're not tired? Or go to a café?' he suggested. 'Anything you want.'

'I think what I'd most like to do is see the house. I can't wait to see where I'm going to live. Then maybe have a bath. I used Anna's rose water – that was the nice lady with the sconces on the train – but I still smell!' she said, wrinkling her nose; then, whispering, 'It has been a few days since I had a proper wash,' she admitted, looking a bit embarrassed.

His heart went out to her. The way Katrin made the journey sound was as if it was a great adventure, but it must have been terrifying too.

He looked at her. His little sister, who had grown up so much over the past year. Now a young lady. 'Of course. By the way, they're called scones – and they are certainly delicious.'

'Scones,' she said, practising.

They carried on walking, and she stopped before a bakery and used her other new English words on him. 'Cake please.'

He grinned. 'There is cake waiting for us at home. Isabelle made it especially.'

'And you wanted to go somewhere else!' she admonished him.

'Sorry,' he said, as she began to walk determinedly ahead. He laughed. 'Wait, you don't know the way.'

Katrin was greeted warmly by Isabelle and Finley who it seemed had been hovering by the window, anxiously awaiting their arrival. Sebastien was glad then that he had listened to his little sister's advice and come straight home.

The two older women rushed to Katrin, hugging her, Finley taking her suitcase from Sebastien's hands while Isabelle looked at Katrin's face and remarked at her beauty. 'Oh, you're so pretty. You have the same eyes as your brother.'

Of course, Katrin didn't understand a word of this.

Finley made a fuss of the younger girl, exclaiming over her bob. 'So stylish, I love it.'

Katrin turned to Sebastien in awe. 'She is so beautiful, why didn't you tell me she was so beautiful.'

When Finley asked what she'd said, he was forced to translate, turning slightly red as he did.

Finley kissed her on the cheek and said, 'I need you to come with me to all my auditions and tell the casting people that.'

When Sebastien laughed as he translated this, he couldn't help wondering how beautiful they wanted someone to be if Finley, who he was beginning to think was the most captivating woman he'd ever met, wasn't considered pretty enough?

'I made you a present,' Finley said to the young girl, and held up a soft cream cashmere blanket that she had knitted herself.

Katrin handled the soft wool reverently, then beamed at Finley in gratitude.

. . .

Katrin was shown to her new bedroom, which was the old dining room. Finley and her mother had stayed up half the night sorting it out. It had a small iron cot with a beautiful rich toile de Jouy blue coverlet and matching pillows that Finley had made herself. The walls were painted a pale yellow, and beautiful illustrations of stylish ladies cut out from magazine covers had been framed and hung. Sebastien had filled Finley in on the sort of things Katrin liked.

There was also a bookcase that held German books, sourced by Archie. And in a box was a collection of new clothes that Sunella and Anita had brought for her.

Katrin was overwhelmed. 'For me?'

Sebastien nodded. 'The people in the group wanted you to feel welcomed.'

After her bath, Katrin joined the others in the kitchen, wearing a new dress. She looked around the room and shook her head in amazement. 'It's so cosy,' she said. 'Like the stories you read about with English houses.'

Isabelle was amused when Sebastien told her this. 'Maybe it's just a bit old.'

He laughed.

'Tea?' she offered.

Everyone nodded.

Isabelle handed Katrin a cup of tea in a porcelain cup with little pink roses on it. When Katrin saw that the teapot had a knitted hat, she laughed. 'I have never seen that before,' she said in amazement.

They all laughed when Sebastien translated what she'd said.

'It must seem so strange after Germany, and your village,' said Isabelle. 'It's quite modern there, I imagine, and, well, we're a bit old-fashioned.'

'Rüdesheim was not modern at all, I think actually this probably seems like modernity for Katrin in comparison,' said Sebastien, and then went on to translate for his sister, who agreed. Though she added that she had thought that it would be more like Berlin. But she was glad that it was cosy.

Sebastien agreed. His flat had been full of modern furniture, but he found that somehow, to his surprise, he rather liked this warm, vintage style.

'Like something from a storybook,' Katrin agreed, looking at the dresser with its collection of blue and white dinnerware, and the cream range. 'I like it.'

Having Katrin with them felt right and within a few days it seemed like she had always been a part of the household. Her presence had had a softening effect on Sebastien, and they saw a different side to him, a glimpse of who he might have been before he'd been forced to flee his country. Quicker to laugh, and to smile. His face not fixing into a frown as it so often had in the past.

Katrin was determined to learn English and was an avid student, taking out her notebook and figuratively rolling up her sleeves.

Within a week, she knew by heart the names of almost everything in the kitchen, living room and more besides.

'It is the German teaching system,' Sebastien explained. 'You learn by repeating, repeating, repeating. It's boring, but effective. It can mean that it is a bit difficult to think for yourself though.'

Thankfully, this wasn't the case for Katrin, who it was clear had a vast enquiring mind, and was delighted that she was allowed and in fact encouraged to ask lots of questions. She did seem surprised and pleased about this. Something she told them was strictly forbidden at her school.

Finley was glad that Katrin was finding the positives in her new life. But whenever she brought up her parents, a shadow would cross the young girl's face, and Finley couldn't help but see how hard she was fighting.

Finley only wished there was something more she could do, though, to chase those shadows away for her.

She was beginning to understand just how hard all of this must have been for Sebastien to bear by himself.

15

LONDON, JULY 1939

Finley awoke to the sound of screaming.

Her heart started to pound and she was out of her bed in a flash and rushing towards the sound.

It was coming from Katrin's room.

Sebastien rushed into the room in his pyjamas to gather his little sister in his arms. 'It's just a nightmare,' he told her, soothingly, while she clutched at him and let out the sobs full of pain she didn't allow herself to feel in the day.

It was heart-wrenching to witness.

Finley heard her saying 'Mama' and 'Papa' over and over again and felt her own heart twist. The poor child. It must feel so strange and awful to be here without them, even though Finley knew how grateful the girl was to her and Isabelle. She knew it couldn't fill the hole in her heart that ached for her parents.

Finley stood in the doorway awkwardly at first, not sure what to do, then after a few minutes came to sit on Katrin's bed and rubbed her thin back.

After a while Katrin gulped for air, and looked at them, seeming a bit embarrassed. 'I'm sorry.'

'Don't be silly, you have nothing to feel sorry for,' said Finley.

There was a sound of slippered feet and they turned to find Isabelle coming in with a glass of water and a sympathetic look on her face. 'It's all right, Katrin,' she said soothingly, 'Finley suffered from night terrors herself for quite a long time when she was going through a hard time after we lost her father. It's not surprising, my love, after everything you've been through.'

Katrin took the glass from her, and took a long sip. She looked calmer, and sleepier. Sebastien straightened the bedcovers over his sister, smoothed her hair over her sweaty forehead and said, 'Try to go back to sleep,' and she nodded.

'I'll stay with her until she does,' said Isabelle, stroking the girl's hair, a tender look on her face that Finley hadn't seen for a long time.

A soft look came across Sebastien's features. 'Thank you.'

As Finley and Sebastien left the room, she saw the strain on his face, from the light of the moon coming in through the window in the corridor.

She had a feeling that if he went to bed now he'd just lie awake worrying. She touched his shoulder. 'Cup of tea?'

He nodded, then gave her a smile. 'Thanks. I can't see me going back to sleep now, sorry.'

Her lips twitched in amusement. 'Don't you start apologising too, Sebastien,' she said as they made their way into the kitchen, where she filled the kettle and lit the stove. 'Like my mother said, when I was little, I had nightmares too.'

He was in the process of getting the teapot and milk from the larder. He turned to her, a question on his face.

'It was after my father died. We lost him in the war,' she explained. 'I used to dream of the trenches, seeing his body there. In some muddy field. I mean, I didn't really know where it had actually happened. Or what a trench was, but I kept hearing about the trenches, and in my head it was like this enormous crater and somehow that made it worse, I remember that I used to try to get to him and the hole would just get bigger and bigger and I'd wake up screaming.'

Sebastien looked at her in shock, 'I'm so sorry. I didn't even realise, I mean, I knew your father was gone but...' He seemed to be looking at her in a different light.

Finley shook her head. 'It's okay, it's been a long time now. I only mention it because, well, Katrin is probably going to live with this for a while. It took years for mine to stop, and, well, until you're all together again, I think it's possible she'll have nightmares like this for a long while.'

Sorrow passed over his face. 'I know. That's if we can get them here,' he said. 'Some days I worry it might never happen, but I just can't think like that or I will drive myself crazy.'

Finley felt awful for him and Katrin, and so helpless. She worried that the kinds of wounds life was throwing at this family were the kind that might never really heal. She wished there was something more she could say or do than just be there for them.

The next morning, Katrin seemed to be feeling brighter and more like her usual bubbly self, only the shadows beneath her eyes belying the sleepless night she had had or the dragons she had had to slay in her sleep.

She came along to the Finley Players' meeting and was welcomed very enthusiastically by all. She thanked them all for their gifts. Archie could speak German and the two hit it off well, and were soon talking about some of their favourite books and discussing their favourite authors.

It would be difficult, looking at this bright, happy child, to imagine the trouble in her heart and the terror that gripped her in the middle of the night.

All that week they had been woken by the sound of her

night terrors. It had become something of a routine, as had the late-night tea breaks with Sebastien. It felt wrong to enjoy that part of the awful ordeal, knowing how much pain the siblings were in at being separated from their parents, and not knowing if they were safe or not, but Finley couldn't help looking forward to those snatched moments alone with him.

While they rehearsed, Katrin set herself up in the corner and watched, clapping whenever they came to a stop or took a break.

Even though it was clear she didn't actually understand what they were saying, they were all a little nervous performing in front of her. Archie said, 'Actually, I'm quite glad she doesn't fully understand English yet, or she might have seen how much I fumbled my lines.' He said it again in German, with a grin for her benefit.

'Er, sorry but I could still tell,' she said, with a slight wince.

They all laughed when Archie told them what Katrin had said.

Finley, however, as with everything, looked on the bright side.

In six weeks' time, they would be staging the show at All the World's a Stage. When she'd gone in earlier in the week to finalise the details, Simon had told them they could begin rehearsals there on Saturday mornings before the place officially opened.

She had got the sense that he was offering this as a way to spend more time with her, and she had felt torn about that. She wanted to stage the production there and she still liked Simon. She had hoped once that he might support her more in her career. But that was when she had believed that she might still have a future with him. She didn't feel that way any more. She had feelings for someone else and, at the rate they were growing, they terrified her, because she was starting to suspect that she might truly be falling, deeper than she had ever fallen for anyone before.

But she shook that thought away for now, and addressed the group.

'Well, if you think about it – this is a way to experience having an audience before we start rehearsing down at the pub next week. This way, we get a feel for how it might be.'

'The idea of more than one person who can actually understand what we're saying is t-terrifying,' admitted Archie, whose eyes were huge.

'I know I should be giving you a boost and saying definitely not,' said Sebastien, 'but yes, I feel the same.'

Finley grinned at them all. 'Nerves are not a bad thing. It shows we care. The best way to tackle it is to push through – but slowly. Aside from Simon, who won't be there the whole time, we'll have the place to ourselves until the staff start arriving from twelve next week, and that should help a bit.'

Anita flung her shawl over her shoulders. 'Actually, I'm looking forward to performing in front of an audience,' she said. 'And you're right, you should harness those nerves – it gives one something of an edge.'

With Anita's back turned, Sebastien flung an imaginary scarf over his shoulder in imitation of her hoity manner for Katrin and Finley's benefit, and they had to suppress their giggles.

'Oh yes, I quite agree, I always felt much more alive when I had to perform a surgery in front of other doctors. Nothing sharpens the senses like the fear that you might accidentally kill someone...' said Sunella, rather casually.

They all looked at her in shock.

She shrugged. Then grinned mischievously. 'Also, if you think of this another way, it could be worse – it's not life or death.'

'Speak for yourself,' muttered Archie. 'My body definitely reacts as if it is.'

Finley touched her heart and rushed forward to give the older man's arm a squeeze.

Just before the group were getting ready to leave, Archie pulled Sebastien to the side. 'I spoke to my brother, Milton, about your case – you know, to see if there's been any progress with getting your parents visas.'

Sebastien suddenly turned nervous. 'Oh? And did he say anything?'

Archie nodded. His face gave nothing away, though. 'Do you have time for a quick drink at the pub?'

Sebastien nodded. He looked up and scanned the room to find Finley deep in conversation with Sunella about something. Her hair glowed chestnut and she was smiling and for a moment he was struck by how beautiful she was. The way she seemed lit from within.

'Sure, I'll ask Finley if she wouldn't mind taking Katrin home.'

They went to the same pub they'd gone to a few weeks earlier. The Wily Fox. It was full for a Thursday night, with the smell of beer in the air and the sour scent of sweat from the press of bodies. Sebastien felt claustrophobic as he got them a couple of beers and they took a seat at a table in the back. It was dark and cramped. It was funny, he hadn't noticed how shabby it was the last time, but maybe that was because he'd been just so happy to be close to Finley.

He looked at Archie, who looked nervous and Sebastien frowned; he'd been hoping for some good news.

Archie bit the inside of his cheek for a moment, fiddled with his scarf, which he hadn't taken off despite the warmth of the room, then said, 'Milton doesn't really have much news, I'm afraid.'

Sebastien felt his stomach twist; why had Archie asked him for a drink if he didn't have anything to tell him? It seemed a waste. Did he just want to be kind? Despite his disappointment, Sebastien could appreciate that at least.

Archie gave him a rueful smile. 'Milton, I'm afraid, is very by the book. So there would be no queue-jumping of any kind with him. However, that doesn't mean he hasn't been prepared to look outside the box...'

At that Sebastien's world seemed to hang in hope. 'What do you mean?'

'See, he did give me an idea. I hope you don't mind, but he explained your situation to me in more detail – when I kept pressing him,' he admitted.

Sebastien felt touched by that.

'And the conundrum you find yourself in with sponsoring your parents' visas,' Archie continued.

Sebastien nodded, then sighed. 'Yes, it's been frustrating to say the least. I can't sponsor them unless I have my own place and if I have my own place... then I won't have enough money to sponsor them. Also, Gunther would need a guaranteed job.'

'Yes. Well, Milton was able to pull off the last one – see, his wife's family own a pharmacy in Kensington, and they're willing to offer him a job.'

'What?'

'Yes.' Archie smiled. 'And I can provide them with a home.'

Sebastien gasped and felt tears smart in his eyes as he stared at the older man. His throat turned thick with emotion. 'Archie, really?'

'Of course. Honestly, it would be my pleasure. '

'Archie, that's, I mean...' He couldn't bring himself to hope. It was such a big thing to ask.

Archie shook his head. 'Son, don't say no – I have an empty, lonely house. They would be most welcome.'

Sebastien gripped the table. He struggled not to cry. 'I don't know what to say.'

Archie reached out and patted his hand. 'Just say yes, son.'

Sebastien nodded, and squeezed the old man's hand in return. 'Yes. Thank you, this means the world to me.'

16

LONDON, JULY 1939

Sebastien hadn't been able to get hold of his parents to tell them the good news. The phone just rang and rang. He told himself firmly that it didn't mean anything. They could be at the market, or perhaps visiting the doctor for one of Gunther's check-ups. He had had to have surgery after those thugs beat him up; he was through the worst now, but he still walked with a crutch.

So he sent a telegram with the news that, thanks to his wonderful new friend, Archie, who so kindly offered to share his home, at last they would be able to get their visas and come.

At home, the mood was considerably lighter ever since he'd told them about what Archie had done.

Katrin burst into tears and Finley wasn't far behind.

'Oh my God,' she cried, 'Oh Sebastien, I'm desperate to see Mama and Papa, are they really going to be able to come?'

There was so much that could go wrong – they still would need to make the crossing. But at least now they had the chance. Thanks to Archie. It was almost as if she couldn't trust herself that it was true. He had to repeat the news, twice, before she finally accepted it.

He nodded, and had to work hard past the lump in his own throat.

'Oh Archie,' breathed Finley, touching her throat. 'That dear man.'

Then she rushed forward to hug them, giving Katrin a long hug first, then turning to Sebastien. The two looked at each other bashfully, and Finley's cheeks reddened as he pulled her to him. Sebastien held her close. She fitted snugly beneath his chin, and he felt how soft her chestnut hair was against his cheek. She smelled of something light and summery. Later he would realise it was jasmine and he'd never again be able to smell it without thinking of her and this moment, when everything felt right in the world.

The next evening, after dinner, Isabelle looked at Sebastien askance as if something had just occurred to her. 'If that was one of the things holding up your parents' visas – a home – why didn't you tell me? I could have sponsored them, I *am* a homeowner, you know,' she said, looking suddenly fierce.

Sebastien's blue eyes appeared overcome. 'I couldn't have asked you to do that...'

Finley's eyes widened. 'Please don't tell me you didn't ask us out of politeness, Sebastien! We could have made a plan, Mummy and I could have bunked together, I mean, they need to get out. We might not have lived through it like you did, but we can appreciate how dire their situation is!'

He looked at Finley and felt his heart lurch. It honestly had been his lucky day when he'd stumbled into the Thrifty Thimble all those weeks ago and met her. His whole life had changed thanks to this group, and thanks, mainly, to her.

'No, I assure you, if that had been an option, as much as I actually would have hated to ask – I would have. Unfortunately, the law doesn't let women homeowners sponsor a whole family visa.'

Finley and Isabelle looked horrified. 'What?' cried Finley.

'I know,' said Sebastien.

'That's just awful,' agreed Isabelle, whose face had clouded with sadness. 'I mean, it's already nearly impossible, and now this – I sometimes wonder if they make it hard on purpose.'

'Maybe,' said Katrin, once her words had been translated by Sebastien.

They all turned to her in surprise.

'But then,' she added, 'it's how we learn just how special having friends like you and Mr Greeves really is.'

Isabelle rushed forward to give the girl a hug.

'She's right,' said Finley, her throat turning thick. 'I'm so glad to exist in a world with people like Archie.'

'And a world with you both in it, too,' said Sebastien.

They all smiled.

Finley wiped her eyes. 'I feel like I need to do something, you know, to say thank you to Archie. I think actually I'm going to make him a cake!'

Isabelle pulled a face. 'Darling, that is a nice... thought. But maybe I should make it. You know, to show we actually appreciate it.'

Finley glared at her mother, then giggled. 'You probably have a point.'

They all laughed.

Sebastien had to give up his morning shift at the printing press in Holland Park so that he could fit in the Saturday rehearsal, but he didn't mind.

Everyone was wearing thick coats because of a spell of cold weather as they waited outside the small theatre pub just off Shaftesbury Avenue, All the World's a Stage. It was a cheerful-looking building with a picture of the Bard's face painted on the wall.

It started to rain and Sunella groaned as she huddled beneath a red awning. 'I don't know if I'll ever get used to this weather, it's so cold and it's meant to be summer,' she complained.

Sebastien turned to see Finley pause in the street. She had been delayed, and she looked up at the sky and smiled as if the rain was an old friend, then did a little dance all by herself.

No one else seemed to be looking at her. Sebastien couldn't help staring. She seemed so alive. Her chestnut curls gleaming in the faded light, her eyes sparkling.

For a moment, he forgot to breathe.

Then he heard Katrin's voice and wrenched his attention back to the others, who were all still waiting for someone to come and open up the pub.

Finley skipped over and stamped her feet. Her cheeks were flushed and her eyes danced. He couldn't help smiling as she glanced at him.

'Cold? I thought it was quite warm,' said Katrin, who was only joking.

Sunella though thought she was serious.

Sebastien got in on the joke. 'Oh yes, back where we used to live was close to the Russian border, and the lake is frozen even in summer, so we always go ice-skating.'

'Really?' asked Finley.

'No,' he said, his lips twitching.

She smacked his arm and he grinned.

'Ice-skating! Now that takes me back,' said Archie, reminiscing. 'My wife, Gloria, hated making a fuss on her birthday but one year I surprised her by taking her to the Alps and after that she got hooked. I think it was one of the few indulgences she ever allowed herself. That and very good Swiss chocolate.'

'She sounds like a very sensible woman,' said Anita approvingly.

'She was,' he said.

The pub door opened, and a tall man with dark-blond hair, who was dressed in a dark- grey suit, beamed at them. 'Finley, darling,' he said, swooping in for a kiss on the cheek, then turning to the others. 'And, these must be your latest victims,' he said, his green eyes full of amusement as he held open the door.

Finley laughed. 'Don't listen to Simon.'

'Just a little joke,' he said, putting an arm round her shoulders, in a very friendly way that made Sebastien bristle. He seemed far too familiar.

Finley rolled her eyes, but she was smiling. 'This riot,' she said, 'is Simon Alexander, the manager of All the World's a Stage. We're very grateful to you for letting us perform here.'

'Anything for you, darling,' said Simon with a wink, then invited the others in.

Sebastien's frown deepened.

'Come in, come in,' said Simon, smiling widely, showing a dimple in his cheek.

Finley introduced the others and when she got to Sebastien, Simon said, 'Oh, you're the refugee.'

Finley closed her eyes for a beat, and looked mortified.

Sebastien was taken aback, and had to fight the urge to ball his hands into fists. 'Yes.'

Finley and the others went on ahead, though she glanced back at Sebastien with a look of concern.

'Wonderful to have you, and... this must be your sister,' he said, looking at Katrin. 'Finley told me about how they've taken you both in, marvellous of them. Good to do our bit where we can, eh?'

'Yes,' said Sebastien, holding back out of a strange sense of politeness, even though he wasn't sure why – the man was hardly being polite himself. 'They have been very kind.'

'Of course they have, old chap. Women, eh, always suckers for a good sob story.'

Sebastien's face must have shown his shock because the other man shook his head. 'I mean that in the best sense, obviously, old chap, it's good that they *do*, naturally. Women make the world go round and all that, eh? Besides, it's been rather a spot of bother for your lot, hasn't it?'

'Just a spot,' agreed Sebastien, sarcastically. Then he made his excuses so he could join the others.

Wondering how it was possible to come to loathe someone so intensely, so instantly.

'You're coming in too early,' snapped Anita at Sunella. 'I feel like you're making me rush my lines.'

The truth was somewhere in the middle, with Sunella coming out of the wings at the wrong moment and Anita dragging her heels.

Finley did her best to allay the tempers.

Archie's voice was too soft and Sebastien looked like he'd been made from stone – which wasn't quite right because he was meant to be mourning the loss of his wife and child as Leontes.

Still, they mostly knew all their lines, which was progress.

Simon brought them a round of sparkling wine as soon as they were finished. 'A toast to you all,' he said.

There were quite a few cheers over that.

Much less so than from the staff who had begun trickling in and had caught some of the play.

Finley caught them giving each other amused looks and felt a flicker of anger; it was easy to judge when you weren't the one putting yourself out there. She was proud of her group. So proud.

. . .

Finley was surprised that Simon had stayed. He hadn't made any move to leave all throughout the rehearsals, and it had had the effect of throwing everyone off. Not that any of them had been particularly *on*. Still, they had to get used to an audience at some point so she could hardly blame him.

Katrin, at least, applauded them, but as she was still learning English it wasn't much of a victory as yet.

Sebastien didn't take the proffered wine and Finley wondered if he was worried about something else, as he seemed a bit quiet and withdrawn.

Simon however was making a fuss. 'You were marvellous, darling. One of the best Hermiones I've ever seen.'

Finley looked at him in surprise. He didn't usually comment on her acting. 'Really, you think so?'

'Katrin, time to go,' said Sebastien, who was putting on his raincoat with a bit more force than was really needed, while Simon spoke intently to Finley.

'Oh, is it all right if I come home a bit later? Archie said there's a used bookshop that sells German books nearby, and Sunella offered to come with, they said they'd bring me home afterwards as he's coming for dinner anyway.'

Despite himself, Sebastien smiled, but the words came out a bit shorter than he intended. 'Fine by me, just make sure you're not home too late. You don't want Isabelle to worry.'

'I will, thanks.'

Sebastien was just making his way out of the pub when he heard a pair of high-heeled brogues clopping after him at speed.

'Wait, I'll go with you,' said Finley.

Usually, he would do anything to be near that smile, but today, following that rehearsal and the way Simon had made him feel, all he wanted was to be by himself. He didn't trust himself to be diplomatic about him. Still, he waited.

From the open door, he could see Simon looking after them with a puzzled expression, and Sebastien could tell he was wondering if they were in a relationship.

For a moment, he considered putting his arm round Finley just to see Simon's face darken, and the thought pleased him. But he resisted. Finley deserved better than that and honestly, he wasn't in the mood for anything but getting away.

As they walked, Finley had to grab him by his arm. 'Sebastien, please slow down, I can't keep up. Your legs are much longer.'

'Sorry,' he said, but didn't really slow down.

'I know it probably doesn't seem it, but everyone's on track, really. I wouldn't worry if I were you. Simon seems to think it's going to be quite good,' she said, half-skipping to keep up with him. If anything it made her look even more endearing than usual and for some reason that annoyed him further.

'Does he?' he said coldly.

'Yes! He said that we'll find our rhythm soon – the nerves are normal, it's just part of the process. He's seen so many groups go through the same stage, apparently.'

'He certainly seems to know a lot.'

Finley didn't notice his sarcasm. 'I think so.'

Sebastien began to slow at last, and half-laughed. 'I think Simon was just being nice because he likes you.'

Finley looked at him in surprise. 'Oh no, he wouldn't do that – he's not the type; when we were together he wasn't all that keen on my acting, and was often on at me to let it go. I think he likes the idea of me being part of a small group like this as a hobby.'

Sebastien stopped walking. 'You were *together*?'

Finley came to a halt beside him. She nodded. 'We almost got engaged, last year, but well, it just seemed that we had such different ideas of what we wanted out of life.' She frowned, then smiled, looking thoughtful. 'It's funny, he's being far more supportive than I would have imagined.' She looked at him. 'He was quite interested in you, actually.'

Sebastien bit back a humourless smile. He wasn't surprised. But he said neutrally, 'Was he?'

'Yes, I told him that you're writing about your experiences – and he has an editorial friend who he said he could contact, who covers the theatre beat.'

'What?'

If Finley noticed him turn cold, she didn't say anything.

Sebastien frowned. 'People who write puff pieces about plays, you mean? Do you really think I want to sit and tell someone like that my story?'

Finley took a step back from him. 'Well, no, obviously not, but I mean surely they would be able to point you in the right direction.'

'The right direction?'

'That came out wrong – I meant they would know who to refer you to, they might have more appropriate contacts,' she said, her face starting to redden.

Sebastien could have kicked himself, but he felt so angry that he couldn't help himself. Simon had made him feel so small and insignificant and he didn't want to have to owe anything to a man who called what people like his family and millions of others were facing – death in a concentration camp – *a spot of bother*.

Then he looked at her and couldn't help himself. 'I can't believe you told him about my articles. I told you that was personal, Finley, it's not something I wanted to share with someone like... like him. Anyway, I don't need his help. I've already written to a few professional news outlets.'

'Oh,' she said, flushing dejectedly. 'I didn't realise.'

He bit his lip. He knew he should just leave it there, but he couldn't help adding, 'I don't need someone like Simon's help – I was a journalist for a decade.'

'Sebastien, I-I'm so sorry,' she said. 'I was only trying to help.'

He glared at her. He hadn't opened up to her so that she could share it with someone else, like it was gossip; he'd thought he meant more than that to her. He'd thought she was better than that.

'You did help me, by listening to me. I shared it with you because you're my friend. Or at least I thought you were. I certainly don't want his help. It makes sense then, the way he spoke to me, like I was some sad charity case you've taken on. He even told me that all women like a sob story – at least that's the way he implied you said it.'

She gasped, horrified at the implication. 'No, Sebastien, I would never talk about you in that way. I wouldn't do that.' She looked on the verge of tears.

He shook his head, he wanted to believe her but couldn't. 'Well, he definitely made it seem that way. He seems to know a lot about me. I didn't think I'd provide that sort of entertainment to your exes, if I'm honest.'

Finley's eyes were filled with tears. 'Sebastien, please – I don't know how he got that idea, I promise I didn't tell him any details, I just said you were writing about your experiences and asked if he had any contacts—'

Sebastien shook his head. He wasn't in the mood to hear it. 'I think I'll go another way. I'll see you later,' he said, turning on his heel and stomping off in the opposite direction. He crossed the street and became just another face in the rushing lunchtime crowd in central London as he hastened away from the look on her face.

Finley stayed frozen to the spot as people walked around her. The sun had begun to shine, but where she stood a puddle of dirty rainwater splashed against her feet, and she felt as if it had been thrown over her heart as well.

17

Finley listened to the radio in shock. The broadcast was all about the recent Nazi–Soviet Nonaggression Pact that the Russians had signed with Germany. There was intense speculation on what it might mean, with many believing that it was likely guaranteeing that the Soviet Union would not attack if Germany invaded Poland, as many were sure they were preparing to do, in order to annex Danzig which they had lost after the last war as part of the Treaty of Versailles.

Finley was sitting in the green velvet Queen Anne chair in the costume department of the Glory Theatre, but her stitching, which was usually impeccable, was a mess. She looked down, to see that her hands were shaking.

Usually Muriel changed the station whenever the news came on. Looked for something more cheerful; but she had stopped that now.

Finley watched as Muriel reached for a cigarette and then lit one. Her eyes were wide as she stared at the wireless.

'It's getting real now, don't you think?' she said. 'The possibility that we might actually go to war.'

Finley felt a wave of anxiety wash over her. She put the

dress down in her lap. 'I hope not,' she said, but even Finley, who had always been a natural optimist, was beginning to have her doubts.

Everyone was talking about the formal military alliance that had been made between Britain and Poland. There was still hope that a peaceful solution might be found and that Germany wouldn't actually invade, but the idea that they would actually be able to perform their play was in some doubt as a result. No one really knew what might happen if war did actually break out.

Things between Sebastien and Finley had been a little strained for the past week. They'd made up, but their easy camaraderie had been replaced by both of them feeling as if they were walking on eggshells.

She'd waited up for him the night after they'd had their fight on the street, despite the fact that he'd got home after midnight, deliberately, to avoid everyone. The fact was he was embarrassed at how he'd behaved. This was made worse when he saw that she was actually waiting for him. After he'd left her on the street, it had taken a few hours for him to calm down, and then the shame had hit. It was quite clear that Simon was rather capable of twisting things all on his own.

'I-I just wanted to say sorry, again,' said Finley, who, Sebastien could see, even in the low light coming from the passage, had been crying. His stomach twisted at the sight. Her eyes were red and swollen. He felt like a heel. 'Don't, Finley, I overreacted. I'm sorry.'

'No, no you didn't, I should have asked you if it was okay. I didn't think of how it would come across, like I w-was gossiping or something – oh I feel awful at how it must have sounded.'

He touched her arm, 'I'm sorry too, I should never have thought that you were gossiping, that's never been your style.'

If anything, Finley had the biggest heart of anyone he knew. It was what had drawn him to her.

'It's how I made you feel,' she said.

He sighed, hating this. 'Can we just go back and start again?' he asked.

She nodded. 'Does that mean we can still be friends?'

He looked at her. 'Of course. I'm sorry I made you ever doubt that. Your friendship means more to me than anything.'

'I'm glad,' she whispered. For a moment he thought he saw a flash of disappointment behind her eyes, but then he was sure he'd imagined it, because she was soon smiling again.

But, despite this, now things were a little awkward.

During their rehearsal, Simon made himself a little too comfortable playing the role of 'helpful' director, as well as pretending to have an insight into the future that he didn't. 'Of course war won't break out, they'll settle this. Chamberlain is all about peace and he'll find a solution, mark my words. No, my friends, the only thing you all need to concern yourselves with is getting ready for the play. Which reminds me, Archie, I have some thoughts about your performance.'

Sebastien bristled at this, but he was the only one.

'This is terribly kind of you,' said Archie, when Simon began coaching him on how to get his words across to the back of the room, which seemed to be his main critique.

'My pleasure,' said Simon. 'Though it's Finley, of course, who knows far more than I do about acting – more than I ever could hope to learn.'

'Oh yes, that's true,' said Anita, who wasn't as charmed by him as the others.

'Anita,' muttered Archie. 'Ignore her, as we try to do,' he stage-whispered to Simon.

Sebastien found himself warming to the older woman.

Anita shot Archie a withering look. 'I meant only that Finley is a professional, who has been treading the boards for years; it's one thing to observe, but quite another to draw from personal experience. When Finley gives advice, it is from the well from which she has drawn herself. She has dedicated herself to her craft.'

'Don't I know it,' said Simon with a long-suffering sigh. 'I won't disagree with you. This is probably the most time I've got to spend with her in ages – who knew all I had to do was help you put on a play, darling?'

Finley laughed but she looked a little embarrassed and Sebastien had to stop himself from throwing something at Simon's face.

Thankfully, someone from the pub called Simon away and he left them in peace for a moment.

Finley glanced at Sebastien, and he tore his gaze away, not wishing to be caught staring. He walked to the back of the room, near the window. He was finding it increasingly difficult to dissipate the atmosphere between himself and Finley and didn't know what to do about it.

It didn't help that it was becoming increasingly hard for him to be around Simon without wanting to throttle him.

Archie saw Sebastien's face, and pulled him aside. 'Don't let him get to you, son. There's only one man I'd bet my hat on to get her heart, and it's not him. Too slick, too quick to tell a girl what she wants and then too quick to change his tune and pretend otherwise when the time comes, seen his type far too often, hopefully she'll see that too.'

Sebastien frowned. 'There's nothing going on between us. We're just friends.'

'Course you are, for now. But things change.'

The thing was, if he were honest there was nothing he'd like more. But Finley and her mother were providing a home for him and Katrin. They were becoming increasingly like family to the two of them and he didn't want to do something that would risk that. Then there was the very real threat that a war might be looming. It wouldn't be fair to try to start something with her; he had vowed that he would sign up and fight alongside Britain if it ever came to it. For years he had felt this impotent rage at what the Nazis were doing, and there might come a time when he was finally able to do something about it, even if that meant risking his life. He knew it wouldn't be fair to get into a relationship with someone if there was a real chance he might not make it back if they went to war. Even if the thought of being with her was all he could think of sometimes.

Some days just the thought of her was what helped get him out of bed in the morning. The fact that he might see her before he went to work, or catch her when he came home, was a light he hadn't known for some time.

He just couldn't see how he could give her anything besides heartache.

18

Sebastien breathed out in relief as his call was connected.

It rang through for ages until it was finally picked up by a voice that was not his mother's. Though it was female, and sounded a bit out of breath, and gravelly as if its owner smoked a pack of cigarettes a day.

'Sebastien? Is that you?'

'Mrs Vintner?' he said in some surprise.

Ada Vintner was his parents' upstairs, Swiss neighbour. She was one of the loyal non-Jewish locals who hadn't let the law get in the way of her friendship with his family.

It was good to hear her voice, but he could tell that she was trying to tell him something bad.

'Yes! Oh Sebastien, I didn't have your number – I have been hoping you would call. Every time I hear the phone ring, I race down from my flat with the spare key just in case.'

Sebastien swallowed. 'What's happened?'

'Oh, Sebastien, they've taken your father, Gunther. Some Nazi officers came past the pharmacy, I think they had a tip-off. They inspected his papers and discovered they were forged, he's been sent to prison—' Her voice broke. 'They haven't told us what will happen to him but well, it looks likely that that he will go to a' – she sucked in a sharp breath – 'a camp.'

Sebastien couldn't breathe. It felt as if his airways were closing in.

Gunther was the only father he had ever known.

This couldn't be happening. Not now, not when they were so close to being together again!

His world started to spin. The idea of the concentration camps made him want to vomit. The stories he had read about them – the kind of forced manual labour the inmates were forced to do – and Gunther was still recovering from being beaten up. His knees lost their ability to support him and he slid down the wall, his body turning cold. Still struggling to get air into his lungs.

How would he tell Katrin?

Stars were starting to dance before his eyes and just beyond the panic another thought came heavy into his mind, causing his body to break out into a cold sweat. His heart started to hammer painfully.

Why was Mrs Vintner there? Where was his mother?

'Sebastien...' she said, hesitating.

From the way she paused, he knew there was something else. Something more.

It was like he was staring out from a tunnel. He blinked, and more stars appeared before his eyes. 'W-where is my mother, Mrs Vintner?'

He heard her swallow. He closed his eyes and struggled to breathe.

'I told her to *go*.'

Sebastien's world started to spin once more.

'She was at the market when they came to collect Gunther. They knocked on my door and asked if I'd seen her. They said they would be arresting her too because they had evidence that she has helped others get in contact with that friend of yours who forges papers, Oskar Meyer.'

'Oh God,' said Sebastien, in horror.

'I know,' replied Mrs Vintner. 'It's awful, I'm sorry. B-but it's going to be all right. You see, I waited, until they were gone, I made sure of it, and then I went to her place, I used the spare key and packed her a bag.'

'Y-you packed her a bag.'

'Yes. Then I went to find her – I had a good idea as to where she might be hiding. I had a feeling that she might have seen the police by our building, there's a bend in our street you see, and when you're at the bottom they can't see you.

'I've seen your mother stand there enough times to know she won't come up unless the coast is clear – especially after what happened when those thugs attacked Gunther all those months ago.'

'Yes,' breathed Sebastien, who remembered the sharply bent road. Could picture the spot where his mother may well have hidden. 'D-did you find her?'

'Yes. She'd knocked on Albert Gross's door. You remember him?'

'The farmer?'

'Yes. Well, I found her there, and she was distraught, obviously. Very worried about you and Katrin, begged me to get in touch. But I told her that I'd let you know what happened. Albert said she could stay in his cellar, and I told her that I had a plan.'

'A plan? What plan?' He frowned, then thought of Mrs Vintner's summer cabin in Switzerland. She had told them once that they could use it if they ever needed to get out in a hurry. When he'd first thought of fleeing Germany he had begged his parents to consider her offer.

'My nephew, Micah. He's a bit like your friend, Oskar, and he has been using his talents to make fake visas. He has a car too, and I asked him to drive her across the border to Switzerland to our family summer cabin. Your mother turned it down before; she said it was too risky,' she said, with an exasperated sigh.

Sebastien blew out his cheeks. Tears were smarting in his eyes. If only his mother had listened to him back then, maybe all of this could have been avoided. His hands balled into fists and the all-too-familiar helpless rage of what the Nazis were doing consumed him.

'I know, I remember, Mrs Vintner.'

There was a soft sigh on the other end of the line. 'Well, they left this morning. I will let you know as soon as I know if they— when they arrive.'

Sebastien closed his eyes in terror. He'd heard that 'if' and his heart stopped. The bile rose in his anxiety. He tore at his collar to try to get some air. A hot tear ran down his cheek, followed by another.

'Th-thank you,' he said, so softly he wasn't sure if she had heard.

'Of course,' she said. But there was nothing 'of course' about what she was doing.

'I-I'm very grateful,' he said, and his voice shook.

'I know, Sebastien. Don't worry. I have faith.'

He clung to that. 'D-do you know if she got my telegram?'

There was a pause. 'Telegram? No, she didn't say. Is anything wrong?'

He made a strangled sound. 'It's their visas – they've come through. They can come to live in England. That's what was in the telegram. There's even a job for Gunther.'

'What?' She sounded shocked. 'Oh you poor things.'

'Yes, that's why I was phoning. The visas are being posted, they should be there in the next few weeks.'

There was a moment of silence on the other end of the line.

'But well now I—' He broke off.

There was a low gasp.

Sebastien swallowed.

Mrs Vintner was continuing. 'I found your telephone number in your mother's things but when the police came back and started searching for her I panicked and flushed it down the toilet – honestly I couldn't even tell you why, it was so stupid. I'm sorry.'

'That's all right,' he said in a faint voice. 'So you haven't heard yet if they've m-made it across the border?' he added. Even though she had already said, he just needed to be sure.

'I haven't as yet, but Micah said it could take them a while to get there as he is taking the long way to avoid the popular roads where there are bound to be very heavy patrols. Usually, it wouldn't take more than a few hours to get across, but he said it might even be a few days as they are going to wait for nightfall and early morning to cross. I'm sorry, Sebastien, we will just have to wait and hope. In the meantime, I will try to find out where they sent Gunther.'

'Thank you.'

'Of course,' she said, again. As if it were what one did, when it really wasn't.

'Mrs Vintner, I don't know how to thank you.'

'You don't have to, son; trust me, making sure you see your mother again is all the thanks I need.'

His face crumpled at that and he couldn't help the low sob that escaped him.

'Their visas should be arriving soon,' he said. 'W-will you look out for them' – he swallowed – 'make sure the police don't take them.'

'I will, I promise, and as soon as I know she's across the border and safe at our summer cabin I'll bring them to her.'

He blew out a breath of air. 'Thank you. You will let me know if you hear anything – whether she makes it or...?' he said, swallowing past the lump in his throat.

'Tell me your number, and I will make sure either way.'

He told her.

'I will.'

The thought of his mother on the run made him feel ill. He swallowed. Mrs Vintner probably felt the same way about her nephew. Micah was risking so much for them, he felt incredibly grateful.

'Thank you,' he breathed. 'I am so grateful to Micah and you.'

'I'll pray for you.'

Afterwards, he sat on the floor for a long time with the receiver still to his ear even though she was long gone. He didn't trust himself to stand; he felt paralysed by a sense of fear and hopelessness. He was past prayer; all he could do now was beg the heavens to help his mother cross the border safely.

Later that afternoon, when Katrin came home, he had no choice but to break the news to her. As she, Archie and the others crowded into the kitchen, he looked up at them, and they could tell immediately that something was very wrong.

Sebastien had moved to the kitchen table but his face looked like a sheet of crumpled paper.

'Sebastien?' asked Katrin, the sudden fear audible in her voice. 'W-what's happened?'

'Can we have a moment?' Sebastien asked the others. His voice felt raw.

Finley stared at him, her heart lurching.

'Of course,' said Isabelle, who'd come in with Finley, just after the others.

Sebastien couldn't meet Finley's eyes. He felt sure that if he looked her way, he would fold, and he needed to be strong.

'Take a seat,' he invited Katrin, putting on a small smile.

Katrin had turned white. 'I don't want to.'

'Katrin,' he begged.

'Just tell me!'

He closed his eyes, then ran a hand through his hair.

'It's Father, they've taken him to a prison.' His throat constricted and he added, past the lump that had taken up permanent residence, 'They are probably going to be sending him on to a camp.'

Katrin turned wild. Her screams were full of anguish. Sebastien staggered across to her and held her in his arms.

'M-Mama got away, she's on her way to Switzerland. She will let us know when she is safe.'

He wasn't sure if she'd heard. She just sobbed against him, and he held her close.

When she had calmed down somewhat he told the others the news.

'Mrs Vintner said she will wait for the visas to show up and then take them to her summer house, and Mama, so that she can use hers to come here.'

Isabelle gathered Katrin in her arms, and patted her soothingly, mumbling something to her in German about not giving up.

Katrin held on to her tightly.

As he stared at his sister, Finley wiped away a tear that he hadn't realised was slipping down his cheek. Then she pulled him into a hug and he fell against her like a life raft.

'She'll get here. I'm sure of it,' she whispered against his ear.

'How?' he said softly.

She held on tighter. 'We just hope.'

19

Sebastien hadn't slept properly in days. He was too wired and stressed. Every time he closed his eyes and fitful sleep claimed him, he had vivid dreams of his mother being captured and taken away by the Nazis, and woke up exhausted.

He still hadn't heard if his mother had got to Switzerland, and Mrs Vintner hadn't had much luck with getting any information about whether they had moved Gunther on to a concentration camp yet. It was a hollow victory that their visas had at least arrived. Mrs Vintner promised again that she would get them to his mother as soon as she knew she was safe.

Katrin's nightmares had come back in full force. Whatever light she'd been keeping alive, trying to show a brave face, had petered out. She wasn't interested in doing anything apart from learning from her English books, and even that she only did half-heartedly.

They were all worried for her.

Under the circumstances, Finley had suggested that they cancel rehearsals, but they were just two weeks away from their opening night and Sebastien didn't want to be responsible for ruining it for the others.

He found it easy to pour all his frustration into his role as Leontes but that was about the only thing that went well; the other parts he had to play, in disguise, didn't go as swimmingly.

Thankfully, Simon hadn't been around much, as he was dealing with stock-take. Sebastien thought that, on top of everything else, if he was forced to spend than more than a few minutes with the other man he might do something he would eventually regret.

At work it was the same. He was lost in his own thoughts, so much so that kind and ever-so-patient Frank had to reprimand him when it seemed he was in danger of hurting himself as he was so distracted.

Frank pulled him away in the nick of time from the printing press, seconds from getting his head crushed.

'Sebastien! Your head is all over the place and that's understandable, but, for goodness sake, I'm not going to let you actually harm yourself.'

Sebastien had never seen the older man look so angry or worried.

'Take the rest of the week off.'

Sebastien was horrified. That was the last thing he wanted: to be forced to be at home with his thoughts! He thought he might go mad.

'No please, Frank. I'll get it together. I need the money.'

'Sebastien, honestly, you look exhausted. Go home, get some sleep – I'm serious, that's an order. I'll speak to the managers about your pay. You're more of a liability than anything at the moment, I'm sorry.'

Sebastien tried to protest but Frank raised a brow. 'Not another word.'

It was pointless to argue. Frank was right. He might lose some money either way – if he caused any more damage to the machines it would get docked from his wages anyway. He sighed, and left the office, feeling helpless and low.

. . .

The house was empty when he got home that afternoon. He'd never been there at that time of day in the week. It was quiet. Too quiet. Katrin was spending her days with Isabelle in the shop, where she was learning English in the back room until she started school in September.

Like him, she had become quiet and withdrawn over the last few days. It was awful to see her like that and Sebastien felt powerless to do anything about it.

In the empty house, he felt like some sort of vagrant. Not sure what to do with himself.

So he just sat in his bedroom, and stared at the wallpaper, picking at a loose thread on his armchair.

He awoke some time later with a start, alerted by a noise coming from the kitchen, the room closest to his.

He felt disoriented. It was much later than he had at first imagined. His body was stiff and sore from sleeping in the armchair in his room – how long had he been there?

He looked towards his alarm clock and was shocked to see that it was gone two in the morning. He realised with shock that he hadn't gone to his other job, and would lose his wages there too. He cursed himself.

He got up and went into the kitchen and found Finley there, in her nightdress. In the pale light of the candle she'd lit, possibly so as not to disturb anyone by putting on the light, the glow was highlighting her rather pleasing shape, possibly more than she realised.

'Oh, um, sorry,' he said, making to back away.

'Oh no, wait,' she said, and put on a robe that she had discarded on the back of the chair. 'Sorry, I'm decent now!'

He hesitated on the threshold, and she stared at him. 'Sandwich?' she offered.

On the table before her there was ham, cheese and pickles.

His stomach grumbled audibly and she gave a soft laugh. 'When was the last time you ate?'

He couldn't remember.

'I'll cut the bread,' he offered.

'Thanks, here's the butter,' she said, pushing the dish towards him.

'Bit late for dinner?' he asked. 'Not that I mind.'

'I was finishing our costumes for the play, and forgot to eat.'

He remembered her telling him about that over the last few days, and he'd stood while she'd taken his measurements, but his head had been elsewhere.

'Should get them done in a couple of days. The group are coming over tomorrow for their fittings. Can you be around some time after dinner?'

He nodded. 'I'll be here all week, actually.'

'Oh?'

'Frank thought I needed some time away from work.'

He didn't tell her he'd slept through his shift at the factory, things felt bad enough.

She blinked and then said carefully, 'How do you feel about that?'

'About as well as you can imagine.'

'Like you have no idea what to do with yourself?' she guessed.

'Exactly,' he said. 'It's not great – I mean, what about rent? You and your mother are doing so much for us, and I can't ask that of you as well.'

She frowned. 'Sebastien, you've suffered a shock. Honestly, don't worry about that for now. You've got enough to think about.' She touched his hand. 'I'm so sorry, I'd hoped we would have heard about your mum getting across the border by now.'

He nodded, then bit his lip, looking away. Determined not to cry. 'Me too.'

A memory washed over him.

The water was warm as she gently sluiced the shampoo from his hair into the basin.

Two of the other hairdressers were chatting at the back and the warm June sunlight spilled through the large window of the salon, making the room glow behind his closed eyes.

'You look like a cat with that smile,' she said. 'You always loved it when I played with your hair, even as a baby.'

He grinned. 'I'll have to marry a hairdresser when I grow up then.'

She laughed. 'Maybe.' But her voice sounded sad.

'What's wrong, don't you want me to get married?'

She made a funny sound, and then she began to sluice more warm water over his head. 'I do,' she sighed, 'but I also sort of want you to stay this age for ever,' and he felt her arms tighten around him. 'My boy.'

He released a shuddery breath now, thinking back to that day. He hadn't really understood what she meant when he was young and had been in such a rush to grow up, but he did now. He would have given anything to go back to that day, when neither of them could ever have imagined what was coming over the horizon for them.

Finley saw the look on his face and came over to hug him.

He looked at her deep brown eyes and then, before he knew what had come over him, he leaned forward, needing her in a way that he could no longer pretend he didn't, and kissed her softly on the lips.

There was a sharp intake of breath from Finley, and her eyes widened.

He broke away, frowning. 'Sorry, I—'

She shook her head fiercely and said, 'I've been wanting you to do that for far too long,' and she took his face in her hands and kissed him back, far more urgently than he had kissed her.

He reached for her like a man who was drowning, his arms lifting her into his lap, their dinner forgotten.

It would be a long time before they came up for air.

20

When the telephone rang that morning at just after 5 a.m., Sebastien stumbled out of bed like a man who had heard a bullet, and rushed towards the kitchen.

Yet, even as it rang, even as his heart thundered in his ears, he hesitated for a moment. He knew it was for him. No one else would phone at this time.

Whatever was on the other side was news of his mother, and if he didn't answer he might never know if it was bad.

Katrin came tearing into the kitchen, without her slippers, followed by Isabelle and Finley, who were putting on their robes mid-dash.

He looked at them in worry for a moment, shook himself, then answered it, his hand shaking softly. 'Hello?'

Over the faint crackling line, he heard her thin, anxious voice. 'Sebastien?'

His legs gave out slightly. 'Mama?'

'It's Mama, is it Mama!' cried Katrin, her face shining.

He nodded, and then held the receiver between the two of them so they could all hear.

Relief suffused him. She was safe.

'It's taken us nearly a week but we are here now, in Switzerland, safe at the cabin.'

'And Papa?' burst out Katrin. 'Have you heard anything?'

'N-not yet,' said their mother, her voice breaking. There was a pause as she seemed to take a moment to catch her breath. 'Did you speak to Mrs Vintner?' she asked.

Sebastien nodded, though of course she couldn't see that. 'I did.'

There was a sharp intake of breath. 'Oh, I'm glad. She'd been so wonderful, and Micah, of course, who drove me here. They've both taken such a risk.'

'I am so grateful to them,' said Sebastien.

There was a faint sound from their mother. 'Me too.'

'I'm so glad you are safe. And now maybe we can be together. Mrs Vintner said as soon as she knew you were she'd come see you, to bring your visas,' said Sebastien.

'What?' breathed their mother. 'Our visas were granted? Oh, my goodness, I feel faint.'

Sebastien swallowed past the lump in his throat. 'Yes, they've come. Mrs Vintner said she will take them to you, as soon as she knows you're safe.'

There was the sound of her expelling a breath. 'I didn't know if that would ever happen. S-so maybe I can come to you soon, after all.'

'Yes!' said Sebastien and Katrin together.

Finley and Isabelle left them like that, holding on to one another and talking to their mother, who was, miraculously, safe and across the Swiss border.

'Oh Mama, I can't wait to see you,' cried Katrin. 'I just wish we could bring Papa here too.'

There was an odd sound from the receiver, and they realised Marta was crying. 'Me too, my darling.'

. . .

Sebastien stared at his article in *The Times*, alongside a picture of him that their photographer had taken of him sitting in a café and writing in his notebook, a place that the caption noted would have been illegal for him to be visiting had it been in the country where he used to live.

It was the first article he'd had published in Britain, in English.

It spoke of his life in Hitler's Germany, and offered a gritty insight into what life had been like for him until he'd been forced to flee.

Finley had bought what seemed like every copy from the newsstands.

'I'm so proud of you,' she said. 'People need to know what it was like.'

He gave her a crooked smile. 'But how will they if you've bought every paper in London?'

She laughed. 'Hardly. Anyway, I thought we could start a scrapbook.'

A cloud passed over his eyes, and he was reminded that long ago his mother had done the same thing. He felt touched.

'Does it feel good to have got back into journalism after all this time?' asked Isabelle. 'Like you're back in the action in a way?'

He nodded. It did. But he also knew that simply writing about what happened wasn't going to be enough.

He wanted to do something more.

Britain was still hoping to avoid a war with Germany. The past few days had been full of the talks between the two nations, as well as Hitler's demands in order to ensure peace. Everyone was hoping that some form of settlement could be reached. But in the meantime people were beginning to plan in case war, did, in fact, break out.

Isabelle thought it would be a good idea to escape to the countryside. Sunella's family were planning on doing the same.

Finley didn't know what she would do; she didn't want to think about it. Instead she played ostrich and planned an impromptu party around their costume fittings to celebrate that Marta was safe.

She bought sparkling wine, Isabelle made a cake, and amid the adjustments they all celebrated the good news.

Of course, it was still muted by the looming threat of war, and the knowledge that Katrin and Sebastien's father, Gunther, had likely been taken to a concentration camp.

They didn't know how long it would take for Marta to get her visa from Mrs Vintner and book passage to come to England, but for now she was safe and that was all that mattered and, as Finley said, it deserved a party.

Still, all things considered, it was with a much lighter heart that Sebastien received the rest of the Finley Players that night.

Sunella, who didn't drink, raised a glass of cordial to his family's health and they all let out a big cheer.

'I can't believe it's almost September – in just a few days' time we will be having our first ever performance,' said Archie, who looked a bit green at the thought.

'That's if Britain and Hitler can settle this issue,' said Anita. A shadow passed over her eyes. 'I feel like I've been on the edge of my seat all week.'

'Me too,' admitted Finley.

Sebastien frowned. He had too, but for different reasons. He'd long vowed that if Britain ever declared war he would join up. For years he'd been consumed with anger and frustration at what the Nazis had been doing. If war was coming, he wanted to fight. He needed to.

But he didn't know how he was going to break the news to Finley, especially now.

.   .   .

But by the first of September all hopes of avoiding another war were dashed, as on that morning they woke to the news that Germany had invaded Poland.

On the third of September Finley, Sebastien, Isabelle and Katrin gathered around the radio in the kitchen to hear their prime minister, Neville Chamberlain, announce that Britain had delivered an ultimatum to Germany demanding that it withdraw from Poland, which had not been met with a reply, and, thus, Britain was now at war with Germany.

Finley gasped. The news landed with the force of a hammer. She looked up and, in that moment, felt her life shift once more beneath her feet, as if it had divided again into a moment of before and a moment of after.

The last war had cost them so much. What would this one take?

She felt her knees buckle under her.

21

LONDON, SEPTEMBER 1939

Marta arrived in London at the end of September, to a country that had launched itself straight into a war, sending troops to Poland immediately after the announcement that they were now at war. For a country that had so long resisted going into battle, now that it had come about the mood was charged with spirit and the certain belief that Britain would be victorious.

They were not to know that this was a feeling that was not built to last and in just a few months they would have to face the fact that this was going to be a war that would take every ounce of fight they had.

For Marta, coming back to Britain was not easy.

Her flight to Switzerland had taken its toll. She had grown thin and developed a cough that racked her body and kept her awake at night as she worried about her husband, who'd been taken to a camp somewhere 'east'. That was all Mrs Vintner had been able to find out, after weeks of investigating.

But seeing her children at long last, running towards her when she finally left the ship, was like a balm for the soul.

Katrin got to her first, crying out, 'Mama!'

Marta collapsed into her daughter's arms, and could not stop her tears as she looked up and saw her son's beautiful face.

Sebastien was shocked at the change in her; his beautiful glamorous mother, who always had the most elegant hair, make-up and nails, now was painfully thin; her hair was nearly all white and, though it was still done up neatly, it had lost its usual gloss and sheen. There were lines on her face that hadn't been there before. Pain in her eyes. Her skin was pale and clammy-looking.

He came forward and the three of them stood in a huddle together for a long time.

Marta sobbed. It had been a long journey in more ways than one but she was here now. At last. She had one little suitcase, the things that Mrs Vintner had packed. There was nothing sentimental. No pictures or mementoes or anything to show for the life they had lived. But that didn't matter now.

She was with her children and she was in England.

'How was your journey?' asked Sebastien. 'You look tired – sick even? Are you all right?'

'It was fine, seas were a bit choppy but honestly I couldn't have cared. And I'm fine, just battling a little cold; besides' – a ghost of a smile flitted across her face – 'it's rude to tell a lady she looks tired.'

'I don't see why,' said Katrin. 'It's not like you're saying she looks old, because you don't, you're just as beautiful as ever.'

It wasn't strictly true, she looked a bit ill, but Katrin would have found her beautiful even if she'd arrived wearing a rubbish bag, she had missed her so much.

'Thank you for that,' said Marta, who at this point felt ancient, despite only being forty-seven.

'Wait till you see your room at Archie's place,' said Katrin. 'We've all been doing it up this past week. Finley made you some new curtains, in your favourite colour, yellow, and Isabelle made the cake because Finley's cooking is awful.' She grinned. 'You're going to love Archie, and Finley of course, she's so much fun. I was a bit sad that I'll be leaving her and Isabelle and Sebastien, but living with someone who can speak German who is so kind is definitely a solace,' she went on quite seriously, talking a mile a minute.

'Oh, that is so lovely of everyone,' said Marta, who looked very touched. Then she looked at Sebastien and said, 'I am looking forward to meeting Finley.'

Katrin laughed, then pointed at Sebastien's face. 'He's blushing.'

He rolled his eyes at his little sister, but didn't deny that his face had coloured slightly.

Marta loved her room. Archie's house was in a quiet street not far from Finley and Isabelle's house. He lived in a blue terrace with a small garden that had a birch tree whose leaves had already started to turn gold as summer turned to autumn.

Finley was sure that it must have been slightly over-whelming for Marta to meet everyone. The poor woman looked exhausted and it seemed an effort for her to speak English. She remembered that Sebastien had said that she had lived here when he was a baby, but that was over thirty years ago now. Marta kept apologising for how rusty her English was. Isabelle in turn apologised that her German wasn't quite there yet.

There was pain behind Marta's eyes that never truly shifted, and they knew that it was from the constant worry she had for Gunther, who had been taken away to a concentration camp, somewhere east. She still didn't know where and that must have been torture for her.

They'd all come to welcome her, including all the members of the amateur dramatics group. It had been a joint effort to get the two spare rooms ready for Marta and Katrin. Archie had been very concerned that it should be comfortable for them all. They had all worked together to source a desk for Katrin and a new wardrobe for her too, as the one in the spare room was falling apart.

Sunella and Anita took over the kitchen and made lunch, bickering often but somehow enjoying themselves. It seemed the only ones who hadn't realised they'd become best friends were them.

Marta and Isabelle spent a while chatting, and Finley was touched when Marta came up to her and held out her hand. 'Thank you,' she said, 'for being such a good friend to my children. All I ever hear is about how much they adore you.'

Finley smiled, then squeezed her hand. 'It is very mutual, they are both so wonderful.'

In the end, it was Isabelle who saw the exhaustion on Marta's face and broke up the party.

She could barely hold back the tears though when Katrin came racing after her for one last hug, and told her she would miss her.

Isabelle shook her head, and smiled through her tears. 'I won't let you, I'll be back often.'

'Promise?'

'Promise.'

Finley was glad that Sebastien would still be staying with them. But she wondered if a part of him wished he were there with his mother and sister, and she wouldn't blame him if he did.

They hadn't spoken about that kiss. That one passionate kiss in the middle of the night when he was so raw and vulnerable. Things afterwards had been slightly more formal between them. A few times she had felt the press of his fingers against her own as they passed, and her heart would start to pound. But he never took it further and sometimes, when she was alone, she wondered if she was mistaking those moments of affection for more than what it was.

He'd told her that he was grateful to have her as a friend. Even his mother had told her the same. Was that all it was? *Friendship?*

She didn't know if he regretted their kiss or not. Perhaps he felt that it wasn't the right time in his life to begin a relationship. She wouldn't blame him. There was just so much going on. The world was going mad.

They hadn't had a real moment alone together for weeks. Every time there was a snatched few seconds, when he seemed on the verge of saying something to her, or was looking at her in a way that made her sure that he wanted to kiss her again, they were interrupted, either by his sister or her mother or a combination of them. It didn't help that Isabelle had taken to staying up late, so they hadn't had one of their usual midnight chats in weeks.

But she couldn't deny that ever since that kiss it was like something had shifted in her; a space in her heart no longer belonged to her any more. It was his. It was so different from what she had felt for Simon and honestly it scared her a little.

A part of her couldn't bring herself to ask him to go somewhere private with her so they could really talk about it in case he didn't feel the same.

Now that Marta was here, Finley wondered if things might settle down somewhat – or as far as they could with a country at war – so that they might speak about what was happening between them without so many distractions. But as it turned out, when they came home that afternoon, there was another one waiting for them.

'Surprise!' called a young man's voice.

'Christopher!' Finley cried, rushing forward to embrace her younger brother, who towered over her five-foot-two stature. He had dark-blond hair and laughing green eyes, and a smile that looked just like hers.

Isabelle kissed her son's cheek and the two hugged for ages.

Then Christopher held out a hand to Sebastien. 'So good to finally meet you.'

'You too,' said Sebastien, clapping the younger man on the back and smiling widely.

Finley fizzled with excitement. 'Are you home for the holidays?'

A cloud passed over Christopher's face for a moment. 'Something like that. Look, I don't want to fight with you about this, and I didn't want to break it to you like this' – he smiled, but it was a bit grim – 'I was hoping I'd get a day or two, but I'm getting posted out in a few days – Poland, most likely.'

Finley felt her legs turn weak. 'P-posted?' she said. 'Christopher, you can't have—'

There was a sharp intake of breath from Isabelle as she entered the room and caught the tail end of the conversation. Her face was pale. 'What's going on?' she breathed.

Christopher blew out his cheeks, for a moment. He didn't meet their eyes. Then he squared his shoulders and said, 'I've joined the army.'

Finley closed her eyes in horror. Even though he'd told her, more than once, that he would join if a war came, a part of her hadn't wanted to believe it.

'W-what?' said Isabelle, touching her heart. Her legs wobbled, and Sebastien stepped forward to offer her his support.

For Finley it felt like a lead weight had settled around her heart.

'I can't believe you've actually done it,' she breathed.

There was a faint mewling sound from their mother. 'Me neither. I think a part of me hoped, prayed that you were just talking...'

Christopher's eyes looked troubled. 'I know.' He swallowed. 'You must hate me,' he whispered.

Isabelle's eyes filled with tears. She looked up, and took a deep breath. 'We don't hate you, Christopher. We just lived through a war where your father didn't come back – and the idea of l-losing you, is unbearable.'

He looked at the floor. 'I know that.'

Finley's lip trembled, and she felt a flash of rage at her beloved little brother. Why did he have to play the hero? What did he need to prove? Hadn't they learned from the earliest age what the cost of war was?

She banged a hand on the wall, and Christopher wasn't the only one to flinch.

'So why do it to us, then!'

'Finley,' said Sebastien, and she just glared at him too.

'My whole life, Fin, I've heard about what losing our father did to the two of us,' Christopher said. 'But what about him?'

There was a sharp intake of breath from Isabelle.

'What do you mean?'

Christopher turned to look at her, then back towards Finley, who was still glaring at him and wiping away hot, angry tears.

'I mean, he risked everything he loved to do what he felt was right, and I've always felt that we forget that part. We forget how brave he was to do that. I think if the man who fathered me could show that kind of courage, well, perhaps I should too. I mean, this is a war we *need* to fight – just look at Sebastien and his family, look at what is happening abroad. How can I not fight? It's exactly what my father would have done! How can I not honour his memory and courage by not doing the same?'

Finley's lip trembled. 'Oh Christopher,' she said. 'I wish you'd told us that you felt this way before. I promise we never meant to make it seem that we didn't know the sacrifice he was making, or how brave he was.'

'He was the bravest man I knew,' agreed Isabelle.

Finley blew out her cheeks, then unclipped the watch on her wrist and handed it to her brother.

His eyes widened. It was their father's watch.

She looked at him. 'This is a loan. The only way I want it back is when you come back alive and give it to me, do you hear?'

He nodded.

————

Sebastien quietly left them to their private family moment.

There was a shadow in his heart of guilt but also determination.

He didn't look forward to having to tell Finley that he was planning on joining the army too.

He decided he'd wait for the morning to break the news.

22

LONDON, SEPTEMBER 1939

There was a noise just outside the kitchen, and Finley turned to find Sebastien standing there in the dark in his pyjamas.

'I thought you might be up,' he said, coming inside and taking a seat next to her.

She nodded and he took her hand and held it with both of his. Despite the heavy weight that had settled over her, she felt a flutter of pleasure at his presence. He smelled of his usual sandalwood and soap. It was intoxicating, and a part of her wanted to sink into his embrace and leave her worries behind for a while.

'I'm sorry for what you're going through,' he whispered.

'Thanks, me too,' she said, and the shadow of what had befallen his stepfather and everything he'd suffered, from the loss of his home to the fear and worry over his family, fell between them.

He squeezed her hand for a long moment, then said, 'Finley, there's something I have to tell you.'

She turned to him and, despite everything that had happened that day, she felt hope begin to squeeze at her chest.

He looked nervous and her heart began to hammer in her

chest.

He let out a short, humourless laugh. 'To be honest, my timing is awful. After your brother's news.'

Finley stared at him with a frown. His face looked wretched and she felt her stomach drop.

He bit the inside of his cheek. 'I'm joining up too.'

She blinked, fast. For a moment his words didn't register and then suddenly they did, and it felt like the rug was being pulled from beneath her feet. She tried to pull back her hand but he held on even tighter.

'Sebastien, you can't be serious. Your mother just got here. There's Katrin to think of. I know perhaps hearing Christopher you think maybe you should...'

He closed his eyes, then shook his head. When he opened his eyes again, there was an odd expression on his face. 'I have been wanting to go and fight since about 1935, Finley, and since war was announced that's all I've been thinking about – joining the English army to fight the Nazis. You can't understand how helpless, frustrated and angry I've been all these years. So powerless... and now, at last, I can do something about it! I can make a difference. I owe it to England too, for taking me as a refugee, not to mention my family – I would be honoured to fight alongside them.'

His words were coming as if from far away. She didn't hear much beyond the fact that he was leaving her too.

Her tears were falling hard and fast. She was an utter fool, wasn't she? Her lips wobbled. 'I thought...' she said, finally wrenching her hand out of his. 'I thought maybe you were going to say something to me about our kiss, maybe tell me what you felt, but I guess I have my answer – if the first thing you can think about doing is going off to war!'

'That's not fair, Fin,' he said, putting his hands tenderly round her face and staring into her eyes. 'You've been the only thing keeping me alive, keeping me sane. I felt like someone who was only half alive until I met you – the thought of not seeing you again tears me apart.'

Her lips trembled, and she pushed him away. She didn't have the words to tell him how strongly she felt about him. How ever since he'd entered her life, it was like he had taken up a space inside of her she didn't know existed.

'You're the one ensuring that you tear us apart, though! I know you think I'm being unreasonable but I'm not – even I, who has been accused of having a rose-tinted view of the world, can't convince myself that you aren't taking a future away from us. The Nazis have made it no secret that they want to rid the world of Jews, so why allow yourself to risk being killed?' Her breath caught. 'This could be the start of something more, a new life.'

He closed his eyes, and his chin shook for a moment. 'I know.'

She could see it then, the pain behind his eyes.

'That-that's why I didn't come to find you after our kiss the other day. I didn't want to do this to you – cause you this kind of pain. I thought that if we stayed away from each other—'

'That you'd stop me falling for you? Stop me caring for you? It's far too late for that,' said Finley, wiping away a tear.

'For me too, I lost that battle a long time ago.'

She closed her eyes. 'Then why do you have to do this?'

He touched her face. 'You know why. Risking my life to stand up for what is right is a price I'm prepared to pay, Finley, so that we stop ideas like his from spreading. I can't just stand aside, I'm sorry.'

Finley closed her eyes. Part of her did understand that, she really did. But there was also the problematic fact that she had fallen in love with him. And now he might get himself killed.

'I don't think I can watch you go,' she said, before stumbling out of the room, unable to see beyond the tears and the giant ache that had taken over what used to be her heart.

23

LONDON, SEPTEMBER 1939

In the morning things were still tense.

Christopher left after breakfast. Finley had been sure she'd cried herself out the night before, but fresh tears soon took their place.

He looked so handsome in his army uniform, so grown up. It was impossible not to feel a stab of pride mixed in with the very real fear that she might not see him again.

Oh how she hated war.

He promised to write and to take care of himself.

'Do not do anything stupid, don't act a hero, just come home to us,' she told him, when he came in for a last hug goodbye.

'I promise.'

Isabelle had made it out of the bedroom, and she tried to put on a brave face, but she was very fragile as she stood before Christopher. 'You better,' she echoed.

'Oh Mum,' he said, turning to her and then rushing over to hug her.

After he was gone, an awful quiet fell over the house. Sebastien told them that he'd be going over to see Marta and Katrin.

Finley didn't meet his eyes, she just nodded. When he reached out to touch her shoulder, she moved away. Her lip trembled. 'Are you going to tell them?'

He gave a sharp intake of breath. 'Yes.'

'Tell them what?' asked her mother, faintly, with a puzzled expression on her face. 'What's going on?'

Finley's lips turned white. 'He's going to join the army too,' she spat out, furiously.

Isabelle's fingers trembled as her hand flew to her throat. 'Oh.'

'Finley!' said Sebastien, angrily.

'What?' she said defiantly, looking into his blue eyes. 'She should know.'

Isabelle swallowed. To their shock, she nodded, then came and touched Sebastien's arm. 'I thought you might. After everything you've been through. I just had a feeling that if war ever was declared you would likely join.'

Sebastien nodded. 'I've felt so helpless, and now there is finally something I can do about it.'

'Like get yourself killed?' said Finley, looking at him in abject horror. It was the moment Isabelle realised how strong were Finley's feelings for him, and she felt her heart lurch in sympathy for her daughter. She knew how impossible it was to watch the man you'd fallen for say he was going off to war and know he might never come back.

They had only just found each other, and, after everything the poor boy had been through, this seemed like yet another intolerable cruelty.

Finley couldn't bear the look in her mother's eyes, imploring Finley to understand, to not leave things like this with him. She didn't care. She didn't care if he was being brave or if he felt he needed to do this to prove something to himself. She cared that for about two minutes she had seen a future for herself with the most wonderful man she had ever met and now he wanted to risk it all. The irony that she now felt as helpless about getting him to change his mind as he had felt about changing things in Germany was not lost on her.

She dashed away a tear, then glared at them both. 'If you'll excuse me,' she said, then made her way hastily out of the house and dashed down the street.

She could hear Sebastien calling her name, but she didn't turn back.

In the days that followed, she listened as if from a tunnel as his plans began to firm up.

Katrin and Marta had taken the news better than expected. Katrin focused on his bravery and the way he looked in his uniform when he came home a few days after he'd joined the army.

The sight had punched a hole in Finley's heart. He'd looked so handsome in his army uniform; the brown fatigues brought out the impossible blue of his eyes. He seemed to stand straighter and taller, and for some reason it made her feel angry, because while he had grown taller she felt as if she'd been cut down at the knees at the very real prospect of having him taken from her. She wanted him to rail about it like she was.

She was still angry and she knew she was letting herself down, and him, but she couldn't seem to help herself.

The only consolation was that Marta felt the same. She understood why Sebastien had to go better than Finley did, but the thought of being separated from him after all this time, so soon after they were finally reunited, had landed as a horrible blow to the older woman.

Still, it gave Finley no satisfaction to see the guilt in his eyes when he looked at his mother. Finley felt like she was in a kind of horrible limbo, where part of her needed to not be around them, but the other part knew she had to, she couldn't not spend these last moments with Sebastien before he was posted. She was drawn to him, whether she liked it or not.

But she was often there in body only. Eating, sitting with the others, participating and forcing a smile onto her face and doing what was expected.

In just two days he would be off to Poland. She didn't know if Christopher was there already. She listened to the news religiously, even though she had no idea where he would actually have been sent or what he was doing.

She jumped whenever the post arrived or the telephone rang. She suspected that she would for some time to come.

The night before Sebastien left, Finley found herself in the corridor outside his bedroom, pacing.

She couldn't let him leave like this. With all this heartache and anger between them. Finally, she got up the courage to knock. When he came to the door his face crumpled as he let out a sigh of relief.

'I was *hoping* you'd come.'

'I almost didn't.'

He stared at her, then his lips quirked. They both knew she was lying.

She bit her lip. Not trusting herself to speak.

Tears pooled in her eyes and she found herself pouring out the truth to him. 'Sebastien, I'm sorry I c-couldn't be more supportive, it's just – I feel like you've ripped my heart out of my chest.'

'Oh Finley,' he whispered, reaching for her. But she shook her head. 'I honestly *hate* you for what you've done,' she said with a sniff. 'And I'm not sure I've ever really hated anyone before,' she went on.

He stared at her and the soft look on his face made her wish she wasn't laying all this at his door. It wasn't his fault that he had come to mean so much to her.

'You don't hate me.'

How did he know her so well already? She didn't. The word she had was too big and too soon and just too much.

'But I deserve your hatred,' he said, reaching out to run a finger across her cheek.

Her face crumpled. 'No, you don't. That's the thing.'

He pulled her into his arms and she sank into them like a warm bath she never wanted to leave.

'I do,' he said, leaning back and wiping away the tears that were gathering beneath her eyes with his thumbs. 'I feel awful that I'm causing you this much pain.' He took a deep breath. 'This is why I was worried about starting a relationship with you.'

She looked up at him, and her lip trembled. 'You knew you might leave?'

He nodded. 'If it came to this. That there was a chance I could fight back. *Yes.*'

She knew then that he had *hoped* for this, even as he had likely dreaded it too. Hoped that one day he would get the chance to fight the people who had done this to his family. To people like him. She wanted to be angry with him for this – for what he was putting them both through for the sake of justice – but she couldn't. Could she honestly say that if she were in his shoes she might not have wished for the same thing?

Sebastien was staring at her. Willing her to understand. 'I know you probably think I have a choice, but it doesn't feel that way to me. I can't stand back and not get involved, not after everything the Nazis have done. I mean, it's never been my way. It's why I became a political journalist. The way I've been living for so long, without a voice, well, it isn't the real me, it was like something in me died. Until I met you,' he whispered. 'And now, I've never wanted anything more than I want to be here with you, to go back on everything I believe in, so I can stay with you, and it scares me. It scares me because for a moment I really did think about just staying.'

'You did?' asked Finley softly.

He nodded.

Her lips wobbled. 'I'm sorry I made you feel that way.'

'Don't be.'

She swallowed, then touched his cheek, then she stood on her tiptoes and kissed him. He pulled her closer in his embrace and her head swam as they were lost in each other.

When they finally broke apart, he looked at her. 'Simon is going to love that he's finally got me out the way.'

'He hasn't.'

'He hasn't?'

She shook her head.

He touched her face. 'I shouldn't ask for you to wait for me, but I am going to.'

'I think you already know that I was always going to.'

She didn't know when she had fallen in love with him, if it was the night she'd first met him or the day he'd arrived with his hand wrapped in that home-made bandage, but ever since he'd entered her life no one else had existed for her, and what terrified her was that she already had a feeling that no one else ever would.

24

LONDON, JANUARY 1940

Christmas had been a solemn affair with both Sebastien and Christopher off at war.

The illness Marta had arrived with only got worse and in the new year she was diagnosed with pneumonia, and spent the next few weeks in hospital.

Katrin came to stay with Finley and Isabelle in the meantime and they went to the hospital every day to visit her. When she came home, two weeks into the new year, she still looked weak and frail.

Soon thousands of children would be sent away from the cities to the countryside, as it was believed that the Germans would focus their war on Britain's capital cities. Isabelle had brought up again the idea of them leaving London too, renting a cottage down in Cornwall for the rest of the war, thinking it would be safe there. They weren't to know that Cornwall would not be the peaceful idyll she imagined, and would not go unmarked by the war.

Marta agreed to go but it was thought that it would be best if she travelled only when she was feeling up to the journey. Isabelle hoped that they would be able to leave in February.

Finley wouldn't be going with them. She had decided to stay in London. She was dreading the countdown until they all left. The idea of being all by herself, living with the very real danger of Germans invading and bombing the city while she stayed here, alone, filled her heart with fear, but at the same time she couldn't bring herself to leave. Archie and the others were staying and there was so much that needed to be done here, she wanted to do her bit if she could.

If Christopher and Sebastien could be brave, then so could she.

Their letters had been the only thing that kept the rest of them going.

Christopher's were cheery and gave away very little of what was happening. He shared stories of the men he was stationed with, and they were always funny, but reading between the lines she and Isabelle got a sense of how terrifying it must all be. Every day they got a letter from him was a good one.

Sebastien's letters were different. They broke her heart, then put it back together again. The first one he sent her, though, was the one she read over and over again, until she wore the paper smooth and, she thought sometimes, the ink seeped beneath her skin.

Darling Finley,

We're being moved today, I can't say where. The men I'm stationed with are good sorts. Most of them are so young that at thirty-two I feel a bit like an old man, but it's funny how quickly you learn to rely on them out here.

There's another soldier, with a similar story to mine, also a Jew, who was stationed with us for my first week, and it was good to meet him, to have someone who understood what it meant to be here.

From the way things are going, though, we should have been brought in much sooner; the Germans have such a stronghold already.

But we are feeling hopeful. It is early days yet, darling, and I have a soft spot for the underdog – and for all our bluster, that's what we are.

It's funny me calling you darling, I didn't have the courage to do that when I was near you, but now, in the middle of Europe, thousands of miles away, under the same stars as you, I can't help myself.

I have no right to call you darling, not after the hell I have put you through. My timing, telling you I was volunteering the day after your brother broke the news that he was going too, fills me with shame.

But still, you are darling to me.

You always have been from the moment I first met you. You have a voice that bubbles with life, like you're always on the edge of sharing something fun or exciting.

I'd forgotten what fun was. For so long I had convinced myself that I didn't need it and then, I met you.

Did I ever tell you that it was my colleague, Frank, who convinced me to join your group? It was after we set the advert in the paper. I never meant to actually join. He told me that there would be free biscuits. I don't know how he knew, but on the day when I walked past the shop I remembered what he'd said, and I hadn't had dinner so I decided to go in.

I was about to walk right back out again though. Biscuits or no, until you came into the front of the shop, I was cold, wet and lonely, I hadn't even realised how lonely I was until you smiled at me, and it felt for a moment like I was coming home.

I came for the biscuits, but I only stayed for you.

Love,

Sebastien.

In the new year she got a job at a charity.

The theatres were closing, despite their earlier vow to stay open, and many of them would be used by the government to show films to the public in a bid to inform them of what was happening as well as to boost morale.

At first, Finley thought that she would do her bit in this way, and learn how to work a projector or similar, but when she read of a job opening for an administrator at a Jewish charity called Relief who were trying to get more refugees across, she applied there instead.

It was her job to arrange aspects of their arrival process, including their accommodation and travel, as well as their arrival packs, which included useful information they might need. She had thought for a while of doing something with her sewing skills, but this was something close to her heart, and she had promised the hiring manager she would go on a secretarial course immediately. To her surprise they were thrilled to have her despite her lack of experience.

'So, might I point out, darling,' said her mother, teasing her, when she told her she'd got the job, over dinner in the second week of January, 'that I was right after all – that there really is value in a secretarial course?'

Finley laughed. 'I knew you were going to be insufferable about this.'

To her shock her mother got up and came to give her a hug. 'I'm proud of you, you know. Finley. You're becoming more prudent every day.'

Finley looked horrified. 'Heaven forbid. I shall have to do

something very un-sensible to make up for all of this.'

'No doubt,' said Isabelle, her lips twitching.

While the Finley Players had been thwarted of actually doing their first performance, they had decided that between all their other duties they would still try to get together once a week. Archie used his driving skills from the first war as a bus driver, as so many qualified drivers were needed for the war. Sunella was helping out in the local hospital and Anita was heading up several wartime initiatives, helping to facilitate training initiatives for local air raid wardens as well as other government-led activities.

They always spent the first half of their meetings catching up, and finding out about how everyone was doing, and the second half they rehearsed.

It was fun, and something to take their minds off things for a little while.

Finley, Isabelle and Katrin went often to visit Marta at the hospital, who was still battling pneumonia. She had grown even more thin and wan, but she always perked up when she saw them.

Sometimes she told them stories of Sebastien from when he was little. 'Did I ever tell you about the time he tried to make me have non-human customers as clients?' she asked once. Her face broke out into a smile.

They shook their heads. Finley couldn't help grinning at the thought.

'He was about nine at the time, it was a Saturday, one, one of our busiest days at the salon, and it was crowded, and a bit tense too. It was one of those wet days in spring when the rain just keeps up a fine drizzle all day, making our jobs as hairdressers difficult, and I was already having a difficult enough time with one of my customers, Mrs Von Ribben, who was something of a powerful matron in our circles – one bad word from her and word would spread and all the fashionable women would look elsewhere.

'I always kept a spotless shop,' she continued, looking at Katrin, who was nestled at her side. 'Not so?'

'You could have eaten off her floors. Mama would run her finger along the surfaces and then she would look up, and I swear everyone in the salon would hold their breath because if there was dust...'

Marta straightened in her bed, a mock fierceness in her blue eyes. 'There would be trouble,' she agreed, giving Finley a wink.

'Now on this particular day, with Mrs Von Ribben there I was even more on edge. Of course she had come in with some picture from a magazine of one of the latest styles coming out of Paris, and I knew it wouldn't suit her as she had a very big fore-head. So I was trying to suggest that we meet somewhere in the middle, and still cut a bit of a fringe, when all of a sudden the door burst open, and the biggest, dirtiest dog I had ever seen in my life bolted inside. He had paws like side plates and they were leaving brown splotches everywhere while he rushed around greeting all of my stylish clients, jumping on their skirts while they cried out in alarm. Mrs Von Ribben looked the most appalled, so naturally the dog made a beeline for her and rushed over to put his paws on her shoulders, perhaps to make her feel better. Then from the open doorway there was my son. "Ruffles really likes you, Mrs Von Ribben," said Sebastien. "I think he wants to get his hair cut in the same style."'

Finley's mouth fell open. 'He didn't,' she said, but her eyes were dancing.

She and Katrin burst out laughing as Marta nodded. 'He certainly did. I could have cheerfully murdered him, there was this tense moment when we all waited for Mrs Von Ribben to react, and when she did, well you could have knocked me down with a feather – she started to laugh, then she picked up the magazine and started to flick through it, and she told the creature to sit and wouldn't you know he did, and then she showed the dog a page: "I think maybe something like this would suit you better, wouldn't you agree, Herr Ruffles?"'

Finley and Katrin grinned.

If anything it just made Finley miss Sebastien even more. There was so much more about him that she wanted to know. Like that funny, silly side, which she hadn't really had a chance to see just yet. It made her heart sore. It had been a week now since she'd last got a letter from him, and she was a bit worried. She had wanted to ask Marta if she had heard anything from him, but didn't want to ruin her good mood.

Before they left, one of the nurses pulled Finley aside. A kind-faced woman called Liz with short brown hair.

'She's getting better, slowly, I think you lot cheer her up no end.'

'I'm glad,' said Finley.

Liz's face looked troubled. 'She's such a lovely woman. I do worry about her, the poor thing. Sometimes she says her husband's name in her sleep.'

There was a long pause. It was clear she didn't know.

Finley bit her lip. 'He's been taken to a concentration camp – back in Germany.'

Liz looked horrified. By now almost everyone had heard of how terrible the camps were.

'He hasn't! Oh poor lamb.'

Finley nodded. It broke her heart. When Katrin came a few minutes later and saw the look on her face, and asked her if everything was all right, Finley only half-lied. 'Definitely, they're saying she's doing much better.'

She didn't need to add to the poor child's worries either. Lord knew she already had enough of those.

25

LONDON, MARCH 1940

At the beginning of the month, Christopher came home for a short leave.

He seemed so much older than when they had seen him in September. His face had grown thinner, more defined, and his laughing hazel eyes were more serious than they'd ever seen them before.

'What's it like?' asked Finley.

A shadow passed over his eyes. 'The war?'

They were drinking tea in the kitchen, while Isabelle made dinner.

Finley nodded. 'And being back here, too, after, well everything?'

Her mother dropped the wooden spoon on the floor with a clatter. She looked nervous. Like maybe she didn't want to know.

Christopher shot her a nervous look. 'It's mad being back. Like you go from marching behind enemy lines, constantly on lookout, to suddenly having to be normal.' He gave her a thin smile. 'I mean, you dream of normal when you're there, you

know, better blankets, proper sleep, eating off real plates instead
of tin ones... but then you're here and that's strange too.'

He looked tired. He rubbed a hand over his short blond
hair.

Finley's heart went out to him. 'Maybe it just takes time to
adjust.'

He gave her a small smile. 'Maybe.'

He didn't go into any real details. What it was like to fire a
weapon or fight for your life. He changed the subject when she
tried to ask him things like that. She supposed he was trying to
protect her. His big sister. *When had that happened*, thought
Finley, who wasn't sure she liked this change.

Later she would come to realise that some of the things the
men saw over there were things they might never be able to talk
about with their families. She just hoped he did have someone
to talk to about it.

It had been two weeks now without word from Sebastien
and she was getting worried.

Christopher told her she had nothing to worry about. 'A
mail truck was bombed a while back, luckily no one was in it at
the time, but I bet you that's why you haven't heard anything.'

Finley felt something loosen within her at last. 'You really
think so?'

'I do. I think actually he's probably going to feel really badly
when he finds out that you haven't heard from him.'

'It's not his fault.'

'We were in the same battalion for a couple of weeks, did
you know?'

Finley gasped. 'No! How come you're only telling me now?
What? When?'

He grinned. 'Recently. Got to know him a bit more. He's
really smart. Likes his poetry.'

Finley grinned back.

'The men all respect him though, he's one of those quiet

ones who, when they speak, everyone waits, because he has something important to say. I think he's probably going to get a promotion soon – I mean, Smythe, that's his commanding officer, pretty much runs everything past him first.'

Finley could picture that.

Christopher's eyes danced mischievously. 'He's got it bad for you though.'

Finley blushed.

The three days that he was with them didn't seem nearly long enough. On his last night, he suggested they go out dancing. 'Put on your prettiest frock and let's paint the town red,' he told her, knocking on her bedroom door and holding out a glass of champagne.

She was tired from a long day at the office, but the thought of doing something fun energised her. 'Are you sure you want to take me out?' she said, surprised, but pleased. 'Isn't there someone you'd prefer to go out on a date with?'

'I'm looking at her,' he said with a wink. 'Come on, Fin. It'll be a blast.'

They had such a big age gap that they hadn't always done things like this together.

'Okay!'

She put on her favourite green dress with a matching peacoat and a pair of high-heeled brogues and they caught the train to Soho and the jazz club, Smooth Cafe, where she used to work as a coat-check girl.

It was a handsome club, with gilded mirrors, chandeliers and low lighting, and velvet-lined booths where couples were holding hands and making the most of the night. The air was full of the promise of life.

For a moment she felt a pang as she thought of Sebastien. She would have given anything to have been like those women in the arms of their sweethearts. The thought of what he might be doing right then, fighting for his life on a battlefield, made her throat dry. She couldn't think of that or she'd drive herself mad, she reminded herself, as she often needed to.

The band was playing a swing number that had become popular on the radio as they entered the club. She found herself humming it, even though she couldn't remember the words. Couples were dancing, many of the men dressed in uniform, home on leave like Christopher.

'Let's dance!' said her brother, leading her onto the dance floor, and she grinned as they began to swing along to the music.

His smile was wide and in the low club lights he looked once more like the young boy she knew and loved. It was good to see him shed his serious side.

When the song came to an end, he leaned close to her ear. 'I'll go and get us some drinks, wait here.'

She nodded, and tapped her foot along to the next song that began to play. It was 'Cheek to Cheek'.

A voice near her ear caused gooseflesh to erupt on her bare arms, as a man asked, 'May I have this dance?' She turned and was about to shake her head, only to gasp. Her heart started to hammer inside her chest. 'Y-you're here!'

Tears swam in front of her eyes.

It was *Sebastien*.

He was dressed in his army uniform, and looking more handsome than he had any right to be.

His face broke out into a wide, almost nervous smile. 'I wanted to surprise you.'

Her lips shook. 'Well, you did!'

Behind him she saw her little brother raise a toast to her, then wink.

'You planned this – the pair of you?'

He nodded. 'I didn't know you hadn't got any of my letters though, I'm so sorry – your brother just told me! I had hinted in my last one that I'd beg home leave for a day.'

'Oh,' she said, touching her heart.

'Come here,' he said, holding out his arms, and she slipped into his embrace. He smelled as always of sandalwood and soap, and it felt like the safest place in the world. Her heart fizzed over with happiness.

'I feel like I'm dreaming,' she whispered as they danced.

'That makes two of us,' he said, then lightly kissed her, there on the dance floor.

She closed her eyes, and drank in the moment, a lump in her throat. Only minutes before she had been so jealous of the women around her dancing with their sweethearts and now she was one of them too.

She leaned her head against his shoulder, and told herself not to cry.

They stayed up all night dancing, Finley and Sebastien together and Christopher with every pretty single girl, only leaving after dawn into the cold spring day, Finley and Sebastien wrapped up in each other's arms.

Together the three of them caught a taxi back to Notting Hill. The streets of London were almost deserted, but here and there they could see the air raid wardens doing their patrols. The blackouts on the windows made everything so dark, even the lights of the cars were dimmed and pointed low, so as not to attract any attention from the sky.

Apparently, Christopher and Sebastien had hatched the plan while they had been stationed together. It was strange to see them laughing like old friends. Good too. Right somehow.

'I'm so sorry, Fin,' said Christopher. 'I almost came clean today when you told me you hadn't heard from him – but I knew you'd love the surprise.'

She play-punched his arm. 'I was worried sick!'

Sebastien hugged her closer, then sighed. 'I wish we had more time.'

A shadow fell over Finley's eyes. 'Me too. How come you didn't get the same leave if you were stationed together?'

'I had to do a debrief – there was a bit of an incident, so part of my leave was to explain what happened.'

At Finley's worried frown, he squeezed her shoulder. 'Nothing to worry about.'

'Is Smythe okay?' asked Christopher. It was clear he knew what it was about.

'I recommended that he have some time off, to deal with his shock, but they didn't see it that way.'

Christopher's jaw flexed.

Sebastien explained: 'My commanding officer witnessed something rather brutal and it's been taking a toll. I think he needs a bit of time to adjust, but he's one of our best so they don't want to give it to him. But it's fine, I'll look out for him.'

Finley frowned, then squeezed his hand in reply. He winked at her.

Then all too soon he had to leave. The taxi was pulling up outside her home and they all got out. Sebastien told the cabbie to stay as he was going to visit his mother in hospital before he left in a few hours.

Finley felt as if her heart was being snatched once more from her chest.

'I hate this,' said Sebastien, closing his eyes and resting his head atop hers. It was cold outside, but Finley felt warm in his arms. The thought of letting go was unbearable.

'I wish you'd think about going to Cornwall with the others,' he said.

She gave him a look and he had the grace to laugh. 'I know, darling, I have no right. Not after I volunteered.'

She snuggled up against him. 'Call me darling again, maybe I'll consider it.'

'Darling,' he whispered.

She smiled.

'You just wanted to hear it.'

She grinned. Then she turned to kiss him.

'Do you two mind?' asked Christopher, who was waiting for Finley.

'Not at all,' said Sebastien, who took off his hat and blocked the other man's view as he went in for another kiss.

They heard Christopher laughing.

Finley couldn't help wishing that this moment could last for ever.

26

LONDON, MARCH 1939

It was a cold but sunshine-filled morning when Finley heard the sound of desperate knocking on their front door. She opened it to find a hysterical Katrin, who it was clear had run across the neighbourhood.

'They've taken Mama!'

Finley felt her stomach drop. 'Marta? Where? Who took her? Why?'

'The police!'

Katrin's face crumpled. She sobbed as she told of how the police had shown up at their home this morning. 'Archie wasn't home, he'd already gone out to work. I thought maybe we could phone him so he could ask his brother to do something.'

Finley led Katrin into the kitchen. 'We will sort this out. They're taking foreigners they think might be Nazis, but I'm sure they won't keep her for long.'

'Don't make promises like that,' whispered Isabelle urgently, coming into the kitchen still buttoning her blouse. She'd also been on her way to work.

Finley looked at her in shock. 'Mummy, don't,' she stressed.

'People are terrified that there are spies everywhere. I'm sure you're right but we can't know what will happen.'

Finley felt like she might be sick.

Since the outbreak of war the British government had begun a policy of interning people they classed as 'enemy aliens'; everyone who was of German, Austrian or Italian nationality had to face a tribunal to see if they were a threat to national security.

Their new prime minister, Winston Churchill, had allegedly said, 'collar the lot' in a bid to ensure that the population remained safe – even though it was quite probable that the process would lead to Jewish refugees being interned alongside the people they had escaped from, the Nazis. The government had developed a system to counteract this but it wasn't foolproof.

Back in September, Sebastien had faced a similar process but had been cleared, as he had been able to prove his innocence thanks to his role as a political journalist in Germany for a paper that was on the Nazis' list.

'Will they come for me too?' asked Katrin.

Finley shook her head. 'No darling, you're too young.'

They only investigated those aged sixteen or older. Immediate threats were interned, those who were not considered a threat were exempt from internment but required to report to the local authorities and subject to some restrictions, like needing a permit to travel, and those who were deemed 'friendly', generally Jewish refugees, were exempt from all restrictions. Finley was certain that this last would apply to Marta.

She had only returned to Archie's from the hospital a few weeks ago; it seemed unbelievable that they would think of her as anything like a threat.

Katrin could not stop crying. 'I hate this,' she said. 'How could they take Mama, she was finally starting to get better!'

Finley felt a lump form in her throat. 'I know. I'll try get this sorted.'

Isabelle made her a strong cup of tea and she telephoned Archie at the library. The line crackled as she heard his voice.

'Archie, oh God,' she said. 'They've taken Marta for questioning because of her status.'

'Oh no!' She heard him emit a low growl. 'That bloody Churchill, like a blunt axe sometimes.'

Finley blew out her cheeks. She felt flushed with anger. 'I know.'

It was rare for them to critique the prime minister, who in most households was becoming increasingly revered. Usually Finley was chief amongst those singing his praises, but on this issue she felt he'd got it completely wrong. These were people who had suffered enough! To be locked up, some of them with the very people who had persecuted them – the Nazis who had made their way over here – was just cruel. There was no other word for it. She understood that something had to be done but surely it didn't need to be this brutal?

In the background, Isabelle was rubbing Katrin's back. The girl looked older, in the weak light of the kitchen, than her thirteen years. Finley's heart twisted. They had all been looking forward to going to the seaside. Would they still be able to go?

'I'll phone Milton, I'm sure we can get this cleared up,' said Archie.

Finley breathed out. 'Thank you. I hope you're right.'

They had to wait until that evening for any news, and when it came it wasn't good.

Archie came to the house with his brother Milton in tow. He was a man in his late forties with tired eyes and a kind face, and over a pot of tea that no one drank he told them what he had been able to find out.

'We're going to try sort this out but it looks like she's been taken to the Isle of Man for now.'

'What?' cried Finley. 'But surely they don't think of her as an actual threat?' She felt her body flush with anger. Not Marta?

Milton pulled a face. He sighed. 'It's complicated. Strictly speaking it's the fact that she was here not long after the last war that has caused her some problems. I get the feeling they think it's suspicious her suddenly being back in the country, right at the point of war being declared...'

'But they cleared Sebastien! I mean, that was the reason she was here – she was married to his biological father,' said Katrin, hotly.

'You'd think that,' he agreed. 'But the government are on strict instructions to take any level of suspicion very seriously. There's a real fear of an invasion by Germany. So for now, she will be taken to an internment camp. I believe it's not completely dire – she will be staying at a hotel, and will be able to write regularly while we try and sort out this mess as soon as we can.'

Katrin's eyes had filled with tears. 'This is horrible! She's been treated like a criminal, after everything!'

Isabelle shot out of her chair to hold her, and Finley wasn't far behind.

Milton looked pained. 'We will do everything we can to get her cleared, but I think for now you should go ahead with your plans. Archie said you have rented a cottage in Cornwall?'

Isabelle's face fell. Finley could see how much it pained her, the idea of separating Marta from her child. Finley took her mother's hand. 'He's right. Marta would want that too – it's already such a risk you all being here in London, at least then she will know Katrin is safe.'

Isabelle touched her daughter's face. 'I wish you would come too.'

Finley nodded. 'I know, Mum. But there's so much I need to do. I can't just think of myself any more.'

Her mother stared at her. 'I'm proud of you, you know?'

Finley had to look away, or she might cry. Her mother didn't often say that to her, and it meant the world.

Katrin stayed with them that night. She looked far older than her twelve years; her skin was pale and the shadows beneath her eyes looked like bruises. Isabelle made up her old bed and she excused herself early, saying she just wanted to be alone.

They heard her crying. It made Finley feel unbearably helpless and angry at her government. Katrin was separated from her entire family now. Her father in prison, her mother in an internment camp and her brother at war. She didn't know how a child was meant to process all of that.

It felt so unfair and cruel and Finley wished that there was something, anything, she could do.

She crept into her room, and sat on Katrin's bed. 'You asleep?' she whispered, knowing that the younger girl wasn't.

Katrin sat up, shaking her head.

'Shall we make some cocoa?'

Katrin nodded.

In the kitchen, Finley put the milk on to boil. 'If we were with your mother, she'd be telling us some story about when you were little, probably,' she said. 'I liked that one about the dog and your brother.'

Katrin wiped her eyes. '*Herr* Ruffles,' she said with a smile. 'You know how my family got him?'

Finley shook her head.

'Apparently he was a stray. Sebastien found him one day after school, he'd got into a storeroom where they kept the sporting supplies. Sebastien was putting back the soccer balls or something, and when he put them in this big box it moved – and there he was.

'He was afraid of humans and took one look at Sebastien and started to whimper. I think he got him out of the storeroom by bribing him with some food, from his left-over lunch, and the dog wolfed it down, then ran away. But the next day after school he was hovering near the storeroom, waiting. And Sebastien gave him some more of his leftovers and after that the dog came back every day. I think by the end of the week, we had a dog – the first thing Sebastien did before he brought it home was take it past my mother's salon.' Then she laughed. 'Mama said it was the only time in her life she ever gave a dog a haircut, and it was the biggest job of her life.'

Finley laughed.

They sat up together like that for hours, telling stories and passing the time.

Neither of them was ready to face the dark alone.

27

LONDON, MAY 1940

Darling Finley,

I have a confession to make.

I stole a picture of you, it was on the mantelpiece. It's the one of you where you're laughing, while looking away from the camera.

I probably look at it about ten times a day.

I can't even be sorry that that I took it. I didn't have a chance to ask you for one. I took it before you came to me that night. It reminds me of the first day I knew that I was in trouble when it came to you.

It's been raining here non-stop in our corner of France, and as we march, trying to gain ground on the Jerries, who are swimming just like us, I keep thinking back to that day when we were caught out in that summer shower. We were with our friends on the way to the theatre pub for our first official rehearsals. You fell behind while everyone raced inside to get away from the pouring sky, and stood there in the middle of the street, wearing your biggest smile. It's just like this one, in my photograph. (So greedy, aren't I, calling my stolen goods mine.)

No one else stopped to look at you, they were too busy cursing the heavens, so they missed the moment when you began to waltz with the sky.

But I saw it. I saw you, that day – the girl who kept the sunlight in her heart.

She shared it with a boy who'd lived far too long in the shadows, and made the world come alive once more.

I hope that nothing dims that light, my darling. Please don't worry about Mum, she's fine, they're treating her well and hopefully we'll get this mess sorted out soon.

Things here aren't as expected. I'm sure you're hearing about it back home. I think we've left ourselves a bit exposed to be honest and our flanks aren't as protected – I don't know how this one will go, but we're all hanging in, don't worry.

All my love,

S.

In May, Finley listened as the BBC announcer told the viewers that the situation of the British army in Flanders was one of 'ever-increasing gravity', and felt the world turn on its axis.

This was not how the announcers generally spoke about the war. Is this what Sebastien had alluded to in his letter? There was always that air of certainty that they would win, as well as a level of opaqueness, where they had to read between the lines.

For the first time, in homes like hers across the country, Britain was facing the reality that this might be a hard war, one that they were not certain of winning at all.

In London, the mood was fearful. A change from how upbeat everyone had been, only days before.

She saw men and women on their way to doing their bit, air

raid wardens and volunteers, and most wore the same look of anxiety on their faces.

The thought of anything happening to Sebastien made her feel ill.

His last letter hadn't been quite so full of its usual cheer. She prayed that he was keeping safe.

Darling Finley,

The weather caused a ceasefire between us and the Jerries, for a while.

It's funny to think of them, huddled in their shelter, drinking their coffee, and dreaming of home just like us.

Do they have someone like Smythe, who hasn't been able to stop shaking? He's our commanding officer – the one I told you about. Well, he's got worse. We lost one of our men recently, and he's been taking it very hard. A childhood friend, you see.

He's not the only one feeling the strain. Derian, one of my friends, is unable to control his anger at the situation – with us left like sitting ducks out here. Strong lads barely recognisable as who they were before. Sometimes it can drive you mad wondering what the point of it all is.

Then you remember why we're fighting, and well, sometimes it's better not to think of the Jerries drinking coffee and being normal. Not when so much is at stake. Maybe that helps, all that hate? I don't know. I know it does something else, eats you up from the inside, like you're fighting within as well as without.

I heard the birds yesterday. Isn't it strange to think that even though the world has turned mad, the birds keep on singing, the grass keeps on growing and nature carries on? It feels like that should all stop, somehow. But then it's us who are mad, not the natural world.

Sorry. I don't <u>want</u> to be morbid. It's become something of a bad habit lately. So, I'll write of something else.

Like us dancing in that club, back in March. You in that green dress that made your eyes sparkle.

I felt like the luckiest man alive that night.

All my love,

S.

28

FRANCE, MAY 1940

Sometimes Sebastien had to work hard to remind himself that there had been a time, not very long ago, when the idea of using a gun would have felt alien.

Now it was the first thing he reached for as soon as his eyes opened.

His time in Poland had cured him of any compunction about killing. Though he would never forget his first. He could still see the Nazi's face. It would have helped if he could have convinced himself that the man was especially evil or had seen him commit some awful act.

He suspected he would live with that for the rest of his days.

Now he was in France, and it had become clear within weeks that they were outnumbered. They'd spent most of the operation circling back in on themselves. Now they were in an abandoned farmhouse, waiting out the rain, with very little plan as to what to do.

He was increasingly worried over Smythe, his commanding officer. He was like a different person. In the beginning, he'd been cocky, and almost arrogant in that privileged, highly educated way some British men of a certain class had, but he'd had a good heart, and that had quickly become apparent. Smythe hadn't been sure about Sebastien at first either. He could understand his feelings to an extent; all across Britain the feeling towards anyone with a German accent was highly suspicious, and he knew that whoever he was placed with was likely to have the same fears, but thankfully their fears had been allayed rather quickly when Sebastien shared stories of what he'd been through at home.

You can't fight for your life alongside a group of men and not form a bond of some kind. Smythe and he might never have chosen to be friends – Sebastien suspected that in his former life he was something of a wastrel – but out here, he had been the one Sebastien most trusted, until now.

The change in him was terrifying.

Two days ago, they'd lost one of their men to a sniper's bullet as they were making their way across a river, and ever since then Smythe had become something of a liability; he couldn't seem to stop shaking and wasn't capable of giving them orders. He was alternatively crying or shouting uncontrollably, and no one knew what to do. They'd lost communication with the rest of their platoon and Smythe's second was a bumbling buffoon by the name of Bishop. It had been on his orders that they had stopped at an abandoned farmhouse, and he'd dismissed Sebastien's suggestion that they do a more thorough scout of the perimeter due to relentless rain.

Sebastien had bitten down his frustration.

They needed to get Smythe somewhere where he could rest, Bishop told them.

Right now, though, there was nothing to do but to wait out the rain and write another letter to Finley, even though he had no idea when or if he would ever get to post it.

· · ·

In the morning, they realised their mistake.

They had believed that the Jerries were behind them, but they were waiting in the village half a mile up ahead of them. They had not realised they were this close. The rain and Bishop's concern for Smythe had made them reckless.

Sebastien had climbed the roof in the dawn light to act as scout. Only to realise, in mounting horror as he scanned the distance with his binoculars, that in their haste to take shelter they had stumbled into the heart of a vipers' nest.

The enemy got up early. He would recognise their uniforms anywhere, along with their vans.

The only way out would be to go back the way they had come and hope that the Germans had made the same mistake they had and hadn't noticed their arrival.

He made his way down and went to break the news to the team, but Smythe was nowhere to be found.

When Sebastien asked Bishop if he'd seen Smythe, he turned to him with a puzzled look on his face. 'He offered to go and scout the perimeter – keep a lookout in case of any nearby Jerries.'

Bishop had pale bulging eyes, light-brown hair and a pale freckled face.

Sebastien stared at him in horror. 'And you let him?'

Bishop looked affronted. 'Are you questioning me? I'll have you know I outrank you, Raphael, and it annoys me that I need to remind you of this, regularly.'

Sebastien didn't bother replying that he often had to intervene because the man didn't have the brains of a beetle. Right now, that was clearly in evidence, as he swelled importantly to point out, 'Smythe is our commanding officer!'

Sebastien shook his head in disbelief. They had been half-carrying Smythe, as he mumbled and screamed, across France for two days. 'He is not well, you idiot! The Germans are half a mile away and you've let a sick man stumble towards them.'

Bishop turned white. 'What? But we checked...'

Sebastien felt mutinous. 'We did a cursory check, no one got high enough. The village is just ahead and I clocked at least twenty of them.'

Bishop looked like he might faint. 'Dear God, what do we do?'

Sebastien blew out his cheeks. It was easy to forget how young some of the men really were; Sebastien felt like an old man at just thirty-two. Bishop was probably in his early twenties, if that. He'd got the promotion not based on any real skill but by virtue of his birth. He took charge.

'I'm going to go after Smythe. You get the others to safety, going back the way we came.'

'Sh-shouldn't we wait for nightfall? Try then?'

Sebastien shook his head. 'They're getting ready to swarm, there's a van parked out front. If they find us we'll be sitting ducks. Right now, they haven't moved out yet, so we have a chance.'

'How can you tell?'

Sebastien looked at him in exasperation. 'This close, we wouldn't have been able to miss the sound of that van.'

He didn't bother adding what would happen if they'd already set off on foot.

As it happened, they didn't need to go after Smythe. The sound of the gunfire told them all they needed to know.

They grabbed their stuff and ran.

In the street, they heard the sound of shouting and a van approaching and made for the trees, only to stop when the shouting turned out to be friendly. It was a passing British regiment.

'What are you lot doing up here, we've been ordered to get

to Dunkirk!' said the driver, a man with olive skin and a heavy brow ridge. 'Get in!'

'Dunkirk?' said Bishop, getting in along with the others.

'We're retreating, aren't we?' said Sebastien, taking a seat next to a man with a heavily bandaged head.

'Yep, unofficially. Not sure how we're going to actually get out but that's the plan,' said the driver as he pulled off. 'I suggest you find a seat.'

'Hurry, there's an enemy camp half a mile up,' said Sebastien.

'I know, don't worry, as soon as they make it up that ridge behind us they'll meet St Peter.'

'St Peter?' said Sebastien, just as a loud explosion rocked the street behind them.

They whipped round to see the enemy van on fire.

'You know, guardian of the pearly gates – but don't worry, my guess is they'll be going straight to hell.'

29

LONDON, JUNE 1940

Finley was tired.

She swung her gas mask in her hand as she made her way home on leaden feet.

Between her job at the charity and going along to all the training sessions to learn about the kinds of bombs the enemy was likely to use, she was running on fumes.

Still, she needed to go to see Archie to see how he was doing. She knew he got lonely and he was feeling helpless about the situation with Marta; the poor man had taken it to heart, and she wished he wouldn't blame himself. He and his brother had done everything they could so far, using every connection Milton had within the Home Office, although so far it hadn't made a difference. Milton hadn't been able to get Marta out of the internment camp on the Isle of Man.

They had at least got letters and parcels to her, though, and when she wrote to them she told them that she was doing as well as could be expected.

When Finley arrived at Archie's he had, rather touchingly, prepared them dinner, and she felt a pang at the idea of him sharing his rations with her.

He was in good spirits though, as he'd managed to get some potatoes, and the scent of a hearty Irish stew was a welcome that warmed the cockles of her heart.

They'd moved on to their second glass of wine when he told her that he was worried about Katrin. 'She's been in such low spirits, and I'm worried that she's sunk into a kind of melancholia. She hasn't been interested in her books.'

Finley nodded. 'Mum says that she spends a lot of time sleeping. She's worried too. I hope that with time, the Cornish sea will work its magic on her and she'll get some of her old spirit back. That and the fact that Christopher is spending his leave down there with them this week. If anyone can put a smile on her face, I'm sure he will.'

Christopher had come home two weeks before on medical leave, after the truck he was in was shot by enemy fire in Normandy.

He'd got off lightly, with a punctured eardrum and a broken leg. Once he was well enough he made the journey to Cornwall. Finley was glad. She wished she could take time off to spend with them, but she didn't have the leave.

'Oh, I hope so,' Archie said.

When she got up to leave she gave him a hug.

The news over the next few weeks was dire.

They had all come to understand what 'ever-increasing gravity' was really about with the situation in Flanders and elsewhere across Europe.

With the Dutch army capitulating, the Germans taking Amiens and then Belgium bowing out, the papers were full of bitter stories about the Belgian king, Leopold, who they felt had let everyone down; but the truth was, the Nazis were the most formidable army, and Belgium had come under considerable force.

And now, a threat closer to home began to occupy everyone's thoughts and prayers; with all the recent capitulations, the British army found themselves with their northern flank unprotected, and it was becoming increasingly clear that there would have to be a miracle to get them out alive.

Finley was terrified for Sebastien. His letters had stopped coming. She was finding it hard to concentrate at work or eat; every time she tried, the anxiety would bubble inside her and she would have to push it away from her, worried she might get sick.

At home alone at night, she lay awake and worried.

The only way she could fall asleep was by pretending they were back on the dance floor, and he was safe in her arms.

She woke up in the middle of the night to the sound of the front door opening. For just a moment, she thought in her half-asleep state that it was the Germans, but then she shook herself for being silly; they'd announce themselves with bombs, not opening people's doors.

Still.

She crept out of bed and picked up a candlestick holder from the mantelpiece as she made her way towards the front door. She shrieked in fright when she saw someone standing there in the shadows, going for the light switch.

'Finley?'

She lowered the candlestick and gasped. 'Sebastien!'

He flicked on the light at last and she saw that it was him. Here.

'I've been so worried!'

'I'm sorry,' he said. There were purple shadows beneath his eyes and his handsome face looked gaunt, but he smiled when he looked at her.

'You're so beautiful.'

She rushed forward to hug him, feeling her throat grow thick with emotion. 'You're an awful liar,' she said.

'I promise you, you're the most perfect thing I've seen in months.'

She'd never imagined that her first time with Sebastien would be on the floor, but when they started kissing there was an urgency in them both that ensured they wouldn't be stopping.

If the war had taught them anything it was that anything could happen, life could turn in the blink of an eye, and Finley wasn't going to waste any of the time she had on false modesty or propriety.

She was going to use every moment that he was here wrapped up in his arms. There would be time for questions and worries about the future later, but right now there was only this night and the feeling of being alive and not wasting a single second of it.

They woke up in a tangled heap on the floor in the morning.

The early summer light was falling on Sebastien's dark features and she was struck again by how handsome he was. When he opened his eyes the sheer beauty of them took her breath away. They were like the summer sky.

He gave her a lazy smile. 'I could get used to this.'

'What?'

'Seeing your face in the morning.'

She smiled wide. 'Especially that,' he said, touching her cheek, a finger lightly rubbing the dimple there. 'I dream of that smile.'

Finley felt her heart lurch. For a long moment, they just stared at each other.

Finley stretched luxuriously, then suggested, 'Coffee?'

'You have real coffee?' he asked in shock.

She winced. 'Well, it's more of a chicory blend,' she admitted.

He pulled a face. 'Steady on. Let's not ruin what has started out to be quite a perfect day,' he said, running a hand across her naked back and making her shiver.

'We have tea.'

'Thank God for small mercies.'

She grinned. Thank God indeed.

But it was a long time before they actually got up to make tea at all.

He told her about what it had been like in France, how terrified they had all been.

When he started to cry over Smythe, she held him in her arms. 'It's not your fault,' she whispered. 'They should have listened to you – you knew he was struggling months ago.'

He nodded. 'It shouldn't have ended like that though.'

'You're right.' Finley didn't know what more to say, so she just held him closer.

At the weekend, he would be going to Cornwall to spend time with his sister before he was posted overseas again. Before he'd come home, he'd been to the Isle of Man to see his mother.

'I'm hoping that they will release her soon. Some of the senior army members are pretty angry that she'd been interned, and they have said they'll have a word. But thankfully she's staying in a hotel and her room isn't bad. She's doing all right under the circumstances.'

'I'm glad. But I hope she can be released soon. Katrin needs her mother.'

Katrin had been going through a rough patch. Isabelle and

Finley were worried about her. She'd become increasingly quiet and withdrawn.

He nodded.

They only had few days together. It was spent in a blur of lovemaking. Finley took a leave of absence from her work and they turned the house into a refuge, waking up early to walk in the park, spending time holding hands, and visiting one of the government-subsidised restaurant canteens, where they could pretend that they were any young couple falling in love, and not two people in the midst of war.

London was full of people like them, celebrating the return of the boys home from Dunkirk. The mood was upbeat and victorious. Ordinary men and women had turned the tables.

It was exactly like Sebastien had said in one of his letters to her about being the scrappy underdog.

One day they were strolling through Regent's Park, where the roses had started to bloom, pink and yellow. Couples walked past hand in hand – men in army fatigues, women with red lipstick and happy smiles – and she told him what her job was like. 'It's different from what I used to do. It's so much admin, helping to arrange the travel and accommodation for refugees, but when one gets approved – it's just the best feeling ever,' she said, smiling. 'I can't help thinking that this is someone's Marta, you know. Someone's Gunther.'

A shadow passed over Sebastien's eyes as he thought of his stepfather in a camp somewhere. Still so far no one had been able to find out where he was.

'So that's why there's this,' he said, rubbing a finger along the shadows beneath her eyes. 'All the extra time?'

'That is purely a result of worrying over you and Christopher. I swear I found a grey hair the other day.'

'Show me!'

She showed him. He ran his fingers through her reddish-brown curls. 'Beautiful.'

She rolled her eyes.

They hadn't said 'I love you' yet but every day it was implied.

On their last night together Finley started to cry. She'd just been congratulating herself on how strong she was being when she burst into tears, only to swear at herself.

'What's wrong?' Sebastien asked, holding her tight.

'I can't bear it,' said Finley, looking up at him, and feeling like her world was about to crack in two. How could she say goodbye to him again? How could she go back to the house without him in it? How could she go back to worrying and worrying about him?

'Me neither.'

She exhaled. 'I think it's harder being the one left behind.'

He shook his head. 'Try being the one who has to leave.'

30

LONDON, JUNE 1940

The first air raid in London came in the last week of June.

The sound of the siren as it woke Finley after midnight was terrifying, and she stumbled across her bedroom in the blacked-out room and made her way to the bathroom to wait it out, along with the little bag she had prepared for just such an occurrence.

The authorities were certain that what they were calling the blitzkrieg was due any day now. Since Norway had fallen, followed by France, which fell in the middle of the month to be occupied by Germany, which had shocked everyone, it was believed that the Germans would soon turn their sights on Britain.

Finley's heart was pounding in her chest, but she took out her torch, her book and her packet of biscuits and sat on the bathroom floor and looked at them all.

She couldn't hear any bombs, but she was afraid to move just in case. At some point she fell asleep on top of a sack of towels, but she woke up with a jump when the siren went off again in the morning, giving the all-clear.

Her first thought was of Sebastien, as it was every morning since he'd left. He was being posted to Africa next. With Italy's invasion of Abyssinia several years before and their declaration of war now, in June, as well as their subsequent invasion of Egypt the allies were worried that the axis powers would get hold of the Suez Canal, which was one of the biggest supply routes of food and other much-needed materials into Europe.

It felt so very far away.

At work, she was tired from her night spent on the bathroom floor. She heard the stories from her co-workers about their nights, and how terrified everyone had been. Though mostly it sounded as if everyone had made the most of it.

Finley hadn't.

She hadn't even touched the biscuits.

The group was coming over that evening though and she was looking forward to that.

They'd started working on a new play. *Much Ado About Nothing.*

Finley felt they could do with a comedy.

Anita was busy with the Red Cross, and Sunella was working double shifts at the hospital. Archie was equally run off his feet working as a bus driver, but their time together was often like a pot of restorative tea for the soul, that allowed them to face the rest of the week.

Then at the end of the month they had some good news at last.

Archie telephoned Finley at work to deliver it personally. 'Marta is being sent home!' he cried.

Finley let out a whoop so loud that everyone in the office turned to look. 'Marta is being released from the Isle of Man,' she shouted and they all cheered.

Finley was an open book, and it was safe to say that to be around her was to know what was going on in her life.

Marta arrived in Cornwall before Finley's telegram with the happy news did. She'd taken the sleeper train and a taxi, just so she could be there as soon as her daughter woke up.

Katrin opened the cottage door half-asleep, still in her pyjamas, and saw her mother standing there.

She burst into tears.

'Surprise!' cried Marta.

Katrin flung herself into her mother's arms. 'Mama! Oh, am I dreaming?'

'No, I am here. I can't tell you how good it is to finally see your face!'

There was a bustling sound from behind, and Isabelle was there with tears in her eyes too. 'Oh, this is a wonderful surprise. Come on, come on in,' she said, picking up Marta's bags and showing her into the small cottage.

Outside, the sea was a bright cornflower-blue, the sun was shining and for a moment, as they closed the door, summer was in their hearts too.

31

LONDON, OCTOBER 1940

Finley set her magazine down. The crowded Underground station in Notting Hill Gate, where Finley was huddled, was full of thick, anxious chatter amid the sound of everyone taking refuge.

She couldn't seem to stop her body from shivering.

She blew out her cheeks and tried to calm down. From the painful sound of someone trying hard to stifle their sobs nearby, clearly, she wasn't the only one feeling the strain tonight. Finley opened her eyes, then saw it was Mr Burns, their postman. She went over to help, offering him a sympathetic ear.

She gasped when a loud blast above made the walls reverberate so much that a cloud of dust began to fall from the ceiling.

They said you don't hear the bomb that came for you, thought Finley. Sound was a good thing in that sense, but it was impossible trying to convince her shaking limbs of this.

'I think we're safe here,' said Mr Burns, seeing her pale face. It was his turn to reassure her now.

She squeezed his hand in return.

They were riding a wave of rising panic, which was spreading. They were like small boats battling the fear in waves. It could wash over you or make you drown. A woman near the stairs was going under. Something had to be done.

Then she heard Archie's voice behind her, telling them that the Jerries didn't deserve their panic.

She turned and felt a rush of affection. Behind him were Sunella and Anita. She hadn't seen them until now!

Maybe they *could* do something? Lord knew this group had been a source of light for her in these past dark months.

She gave him a signal, and then gathered her courage and stood up as she

began to recite their poem, the others following to perform each verse, as they had so often done in private in the past.

When the all clear was sounded, Finley and the rest of the group felt like they had conquered something together. Never had they been more grateful to see the dawning of a new day or more determined to do what they could for their friends and neighbours when night fell.

After that first night, they returned every evening thereafter to perform in the shelter for them.

32

LONDON, OCTOBER 1940

Finley opened the door and saw a young boy holding out a telegram and felt her world turn on its axis. Telegram boys were known as the angels of death because of what they delivered: news no one wanted to hear.

'N-no,' she said, weakly, taking a step back.

Next to the boy was Mr Burns, her regular postman. 'I was making my rounds when I saw John here coming to your door, so I thought I'd offer some support if you need it.'

He looked grim. 'Finley, love, I'm so sorry,' he whispered.

The boy was holding out the telegram for her but she refused to take it.

'It's alright, John, I'll take it for Miss Finley, and stay with her a moment.'

The boy nodded, then tipped his hat to her. 'I'm sorry, Mam,' he said, departing.

Finley felt her knees turn to jelly.

'Come on, love, let's go inside,' said Mr Burns.

Finley nodded, grateful that he was there, that he had been delivering at the same time as the telegram boy.

'Shall I open it for you?' he asked, after he'd led her to the kitchen, and she had taken a seat.

He'd been inside for countless cups of tea in the past.

Finley nodded. It could only be Sebastien. Christopher was still in Cornwall, recovering. She thought she might be sick. The world started to spin.

She heard his voice from a tunnel.

'It's not as bad as it seems,' he said nervously.

She looked up in hope, but didn't find any in the old man's eyes. He was lying.

'It says Sebastien Raphael is missing in action in North Africa.'

She blinked, then felt a hot tear slip down her cheek, then another. Can a person cry without realising it? At some point her legs gave out and Mr Burns reached for her and led her to a chair inside her own home. 'I'll make you a cup of strong tea,' he said.

She didn't hear him.

She couldn't. Not past the buzzing in her own ears.

'Was he— I mean is he... your young man?'

She nodded. Noticed his use of the past tense with horror.

'D-do you think it means... could he be...?' She didn't know how to ask, she had already seen it on his face.

Mr Burns seemed to guess what she was saying. 'I don't know, Prudence, he could very well be alive. It does happen.'

His tone implied this was rare. For sweet, optimistic Mr Burns to sound so unsure somehow made it all the worse. She knew on some level he was likely just trying not to give her false hope.

She blinked. But was it false? Missing wasn't dead. She would try not to think the worst. Her hands shook.

She tried to gather her thoughts, but they were scattered. He'd said he'd ask her when he knew he was coming home.

Those were the last words he'd spoken to her before he left all those months ago... and now he might never come home.

She let out a low, feral cry.

Someone would have to tell his mother and Katrin. The thought made her hunch over and begin sobbing in earnest.

Marta had only just made it to Cornwall.

They'd finally found some happiness. Marta had been in good spirits, as had Katrin, who had begun to seem more like her old self. Archie had sent her a parcel of books. Marta had put on a little weight, so Isabelle said, and given them all a good haircut, and the three of them had been making the most of the good weather, swimming in the sea apparently, and Katrin had made friends with the neighbour and his dog.

It seemed so cruel to take that new-found happiness away from them.

'Is there someone I can call?' asked Mr Burns, who was hovering over her like a concerned mother hen.

'My mother doesn't have a phone,' she said.

'Your group?'

'Archie,' she said. 'Could you call Archie?'

'Yes.'

Archie came over as soon as he could.

When she looked up, she smiled, in a sad way that made him reach over to her and give her a hug. It was a funny old world sometimes. She had never imagined that one day her best friend in all the world would be a 67-year-old librarian.

But there it was.

'He's gone missing, Archie,' she told him. 'I thought we would get married – me, who never wanted to get married. I met him, and the idea of being without him seemed impossible.' Her face crumpled. 'It still does.'

'Oh Finley,' he said, 'I'm so sorry.'

She closed her eyes, and saw him, that night at the jazz club, in his uniform, his impossible blue eyes and the way he looked at her, that smile that only came to his face when he was staring at her. Would she never see that again? The thought was devastating and she couldn't help the tears from falling.

Archie sat beside her. 'You'll get through this, Finley. I know it feels like you won't, but trust me, you will.'

33

CORNWALL, NOVEMBER 1940

The whistle blew as the train pulled into the station in a cloud of steam. Finley stepped off the platform at Truro, into the biting cold.

Finley shifted her bag in her hands and searched the crowd for her mother's face. She found her wrapped in a scarlet coat with a green scarf, the only colour in the grey day.

'Finley,' Isabelle cried, holding her close.

Finley sank into her mother's arms, feeling comforted for the first time in weeks. It had been heartbreaking to tell them the news about Sebastien via telegram.

Her mother had called her the day after they'd received it, and told her to come. 'Finley, it's no good you being there, waiting by the door for a letter that might not arrive. I know you love him. I know your heart is broken, and that is why you need to be with us.'

Finley had sobbed. 'H-how did you know?'

'Oh darling, I knew you had fallen for that lovely man the day he moved in.'

Finley had breathed in sharply. It was true. She had been falling for him ever since they met.

Now she was here in Cornwall. In the distance, the Helford River was shrouded in a grey mist, and she couldn't help but feel that it was a match for the winter that had become her soul.

'Where are Marta and Katrin?'

'They're back at the house. We aren't far, just over an hour away. A neighbour offered to drive me down to fetch you.'

Finley nodded.

'How are they doing?'

Isabelle sighed. 'They're all right – the news was a shock, obviously, but Marta is determined not to think the worst, and we've been taking our cues from her.'

Finley swallowed. Isabelle clutched her hand. 'I think that would be wise for you too. We don't know that he's dead.'

Finley nodded. Her lips shook and she blew out her cheeks to try not to fall apart.

They drove down narrow hedge-lined roads, where it was difficult to see much of the scenery for the verdant growth.

At last they arrived in St Ives and at the cottage Isabelle had rented on the side of town that was known as Upalong. It was a pretty whitewashed terrace with late-blooming roses trailing over the walls.

Christopher, Marta and Katrin were waiting at the door and they all rushed forward to hug her. It was so good to see her brother, who was looking well, despite his crutch; he had the biggest smile for her. Katrin was also looking better than the last time Finley had seen her, as was Marta. Despite their current grief, it seemed being in Cornwall had been good for all of them. She was glad of that.

As Christopher, Katrin and her mother went inside, Katrin offering to carry her bag, Marta grabbed her arm and held her back, an odd look stealing over her face. Finley watched as the others went on ahead. She turned to look at Marta, expecting her to say something about Sebastien. Maybe to tell her not to give up hope. Instead the older woman was looking at her in shock.

'Is-is there something wrong?'

Marta half smiled. Her eyes were huge. 'You're pregnant.'

Finley felt the world begin to rush at her ears. 'What?' She blinked at the other woman in utter shock. 'N-no,' she denied.

'I worked in a salon for years, and I saw a lot of women – I can always tell.'

'How?' asked Finley, her heart thudding in her chest. She looked down at her stomach.

Marta shook her head. 'It's the face, I can't tell you exactly but there's a roundness, a look to the hair – I just can tell.'

Finley swallowed, then felt a rising sense of panic. It had been there at the back of her mind, a tiny niggle that she had tried to ignore, ever since her periods had stopped; but then a lot of women had stopped menstruating from the stress of war, and she had thought that it had to be the case for her too.

Marta's smile widened. 'It's wonderful.'

Finley's lips wobbled. It didn't feel wonderful to her. She'd already lived through a version of this with her mother. She didn't want to raise a child without its father.

But Marta was ushering her inside and making a fuss of her, and Finley followed after her in shock. 'Marta,' she whispered. 'Please don't say anything to the others, not yet.'

Marta squeezed her arm. 'Of course, darling girl. Just between us for now.'

The cottage was sparsely decorated, but cosy and warm thanks to a wood-burning stove. Finley was shown to her room, which had a distant view of the sea, grey and stormy at present like the jumble of thoughts that were swirling in her mind.

They had a light supper, and then Finley excused herself,

saying that she was tired. It wasn't a lie. She was exhausted and had been for some time.

She'd thought it was due to the constant feelings of grief and worry that had settled over her heart ever since Sebastien had gone missing.

Marta's words repeated themselves in her mind.

She couldn't be though.

In the morning, she looked at herself naked in the bathroom mirror and looked at the small bump around her stomach. She was very thin but it was distinct. She must have been fooling herself, she realised now, staring at herself.

She touched it with a shaking hand, feeling an intense mix of emotions, from wonder to fear and grief and love.

She got dressed slowly. She was feeling ill, and she wondered if it was morning sickness or dread at the thought of telling her mother. She would, she decided, but perhaps not just yet.

Soon.

She took out her copy of Shaw's plays, and went down to the living room to read. Arrogant Professor Higgins getting taken down a notch by Eliza Doolittle always made her feel better.

She thought she might do the voices for Katrin, who loved to see her perform.

At least for a little while, they could chase away some of the shadows that circled them.

34

CORNWALL, DECEMBER 1940

Finley knew when the telegram boy was making his way to Upalong by the sound of his bicycle, and she couldn't help the jolt of adrenalin and fear that washed over her whenever she did.

Telegram boys only delivered bad news.

But so far the only post they had received were Christmas cards. Still, it didn't stop her jumping at the sound of the bike, as unfortunately their regular post was also delivered by someone who used a bicycle, and she knew Marta and Katrin were just the same.

Katrin was prone to bursting into tears, every so often, at the thought that she might never see her brother again. When the tears came, so did the accompanying welling of emotion for her father, who they'd had so little news of since he was imprisoned, beyond the fact that he'd been transported to a camp, some-where 'east'.

Marta surprised her. She was stoic, but positive. A rock for them all, when Finley felt that she wished she could have been that for them instead. 'I feel like I would know if my son was gone,' said Marta. 'Here, in my heart. And I don't.'

Finley tried to take solace in her words, and to believe them. She was the girl who always looked on the brighter side of life. But she was finding it difficult now. She knew, from experience, that no one ever truly felt as if those they loved were gone. When she was little, her mother used to always say that she felt her father nearby. She wanted desperately to believe in Marta's intuition but she didn't know if she really could trust it. The worst part of it all was knowing that Sebastien would hate that Finley's light had begun to dim, so she tried her hardest to be that girl, the one he'd fallen for, even though some days that felt like a losing battle.

Every day she woke up with a new goal, and that was to keep her side up, and paint on a brave face; and that was what she did. She suggested fun things for them all to do.

Performing plays was often a good one. Katrin had taken a keen interest in acting and Christopher was no stranger to putting on a production for their mother.

They acted out *Pygmalion* for Marta and Isabelle's amusement.

They also went on long walks with Marta, often accompanied by their neighbour's dog, Robert, a grumpy border terrier who had for some reason taken a fancy to Finley.

The sea air, the company and the friendship of the dog helped. Still, it took Finley time to work up the courage to tell her mother that she was pregnant and that she hadn't been very sensible about things at all.

'I have something I need to tell you, Mum,' she said, one evening while the two of them were doing the dishes.

Isabelle looked at her. Then she put down the sponge. 'I think I might know.'

Finley swallowed. 'You do?'

Her mother's eyes strayed towards her middle and she nodded.

Tears started in Finley's eyes. 'I'm sorry, Mum. I didn't want to be like this – with me being unmarried.' She swallowed. 'I know you always struggle with me not being overly sensible about things.'

'Oh darling, it's a war, you two love each other. I can't honestly blame you. It's not ideal, of course – for you – but we'll make it work. I know this isn't how you wanted it to be, a sort of history-repeating-itself version like of what happened with me and Christopher after your father passed, but you won't do this alone. I'm here, and Marta, and the others, we'll help you get through this, and well, at least you'll always have a small part of him.'

Hot tears coursed down her face as she hugged her mother. She wanted to rage, though, that she didn't want it to be this way, that this was the very thing she had been terrified of – of spending her life without the man she loved – but she couldn't find the words. Her mother held on tightly as she sobbed, and Finley knew she didn't have to say it aloud for her to understand.

Archie had said he would come down for Christmas, and that was something to look forward to.

Christopher lifted her spirits by taking her mind off things as much as he could, chasing around the room after Robert the terrier, who had taken to stealing his crutch, and his chair whenever he wasn't sitting in it, and glaring at him when Christopher tried to fight for his space, in such a human way that they would all be howling. Robert's owner Tommy Slopes, a kind-faced gentleman with a thick Cornish accent, had taken to standing at the living room window every evening; he would tap his wrist a few times, then wag a finger, and the laughter would start again as Robert sighed and reluctantly took his leave of them. It was all in good fun. Tommy was glad that Robert had found some friends, and said he found it difficult to walk the dog on cold December days.

Her mother had asked her, as they were out on one of their walks, 'I just wondered darling, why didn't you and Sebastien get married – so many young couples are in a rush to do it these days? Marta asked me, too, and I couldn't say.'

Finley closed her eyes for a moment. 'We spoke about it. But I – well, it was my fault really that we didn't. I didn't want to get married until I knew he was home for good.'

'Oh, Finley.'

Finley bit her top lip and tried not to cry as a memory of one of their last moments together flashed before her.

They were sitting in the kitchen, alone in the house, drinking tea in just their underwear, when he turned to her. The morning light streaming through the kitchen made his blue eyes bluer still. 'So, I've been thinking.'

She'd put her pale-green porcelain cup down on the scrubbed wooden table. 'This thinking thing, does it hurt?'

He rolled his eyes at her.

'Sorry,' she said. 'Continue.'

'Well, what I was thinking... is that we could go to the registry office and get a marriage licence.'

Finley frowned, then crossed her arms. 'Is that your way of proposing to me, Sebastien Raphael?'

He ran a hand nervously through his hair. 'No, well, how I wanted to propose would have been over dinner somewhere lovely, and with my grandmother's ring, and you in that green dress I love.'

She blinked. He had actually thought about this.

'That's how I would have planned it. Or was going to, but then last night...'

She blushed. Last night they had let the world and all its rules fade away, as they had spent it in each other's arms.

'You don't have to marry me just because we made love.'

'I know that.'

She looked at the floor, and her bare feet.

He picked up her hand. 'Finley, I have wanted to marry you since that first day I met you. All I remember thinking is that you are what home might look like, and I was gone.'

She bit her lip, tears shimmering in her eyes.

'Say yes,' he said.

She shook her head and he let go of her hand.

He looked hurt, and she reached back for it. 'I want to marry you too, God, it's pathetic how much, Sebastien, it's all I think about, the idea of being your wife, of being yours.'

He looked at her, his eyes searching. 'Then let's do it!'

'No,' she said, her lip quivering.

He blinked. 'Why not?'

'Because when I marry you, I want to know that you're going to be staying. We don't know what the future will hold but I don't want to be a war widow, Sebastien, I want a life with you. So I'll only say yes when I know you're home safe.'

He blew out his cheeks, then leaned his head on top of hers. 'If anything happened to me, you could get a pension if we were married.'

She pulled away. 'I don't want that. I just want you.'

He kissed her then, fiercely, and they spoke no more of it.

She couldn't regret that decision, even though there was now a child involved.

It had felt right, even though right now, in her situation, it would have made things more respectable in a way. There were still people who frowned at such things, and would judge her for what she had done. It hadn't been sensible, but then she had never placed too much value on that anyway.

What mattered were the people in her life who didn't

judge, who knew the truth; she couldn't waste her time on people who lived their lives so wrapped up in propriety that they forgot to live in the first place.

Do nothing small, least of all life, her father's motto, was always the rallying cry for this.

At Christmas, Archie came to stay. Somehow, he had managed to get a chicken, and they had a roast with potatoes, carrots and pumpkin by saving up their rations, and lunch felt like a feast.

For the first time in weeks Finley found herself laughing and enjoying herself.

They had made each other presents, some better than others. Christopher's attempt at making a replica of Robert the dog for Finley out of brown felted wool, marbles for eyes and an old mop made them all laugh so hard that Archie said he was in danger of dislocating something.

When the new year came round, Finley had stopped jumping in fright whenever she heard the sound of a bicycle as it was usually just the postie cycling past, not a telegram boy with bad news, so she told herself to sit calmly, as it was, more often than not, nothing to worry about.

So it was with shock when one day she heard Marta begin to scream. There was the sound of barking, and the crashing of doors, as others rushed towards her.

Finley ran to the dim corridor, where the open doorway shone its grey morning light, and saw the boy in the frame then felt her knees go weak as she saw the telegram in Marta's hands.

The blood began to rush in her ears.

Katrin was wrestling the envelope from her mother's hands and opening it. Marta's eyes were huge and full of fear.

Christopher shuffled into the crowded doorway, and put his hand on her shoulder in support.

They all held their breath as Katrin opened it, her small fingers shaking. Her eyes scanned the contents of the letter but she didn't say anything. She blinked, and looked confused.

Marta's lips quivered. 'W-what does it say?'

Katrin looked up at her, and then at Finley, frozen in the doorway. Her young face looked shocked. 'H-he's alive.'

Finley felt her knees give out.

35

KENT, JANUARY 1941

Sebastien had been taken to a military hospital.

He'd been in a convoy of vans that had driven over a land-mine. For weeks they had assumed that he was someone else, because he was so badly injured, his face unrecognisable. He was also carrying someone else's possessions. It was a letter for his first mate's sweetheart that he'd promised to deliver.

It was only in the past week or so, when he'd finally started to become well enough to speak, that they had realised who he really was.

The doctors warned them that he was badly burned and injured. Even so, it was worse than they might have imagined. When the nurse moved aside the screen, Finley wasn't the only one to gasp as they finally saw him lying on the hospital bed, that grey morning in January. He was covered in bandages. His face was swollen and several deep jagged welts crossed over it, like fault lines on a map. The skin below his neck looked badly burnt and raw, and both legs were in plaster. He blinked up at them, and tried to smile, only to wince.

Finley rushed forward to help him as he attempted to sit up.

When she made to move away she couldn't, he was holding on so tightly.

Her lips shook.

'I know I look awful, I'm sorry,' he whispered.

She shook her head. 'You are the most beautiful thing to me,' she assured him, and had to stop herself from sobbing on the poor man's broken body.

She stepped out of the way as Marta and Katrin rushed forward to speak with him, watching with her heart in her mouth as they clucked around him like a pair of hens. 'Oh Sebastien, are you sore – where doesn't it hurt?' cried Katrin, who seemed almost like her old self now that she knew he was safe; she was full of chatter, and wanting to know everything about his time away.

'Don't wear him out, child,' said Marta, coming forward to run a hand through his hair. His eyes closed in pleasure for a moment at the touch.

All too soon a nurse came and told them that he needed his rest and that they could come back the following morning.

Finley lingered, hating the idea of leaving so soon, and the nurse looked sympathetic. 'I'm sorry, lovely, but he needs his rest.'

Finley nodded, and reluctantly followed the others out.

The next morning when they were shown into the room, Marta squeezed Finley's hand, and gave her a look. She took that to mean that was her cue to tell Sebastien about the baby. She had been careful to make sure her bump wasn't obvious, wearing baggy clothes to conceal it, as she wanted to tell him first.

Then Marta said they would give the two of them some time alone. Katrin resisted at first, but was reluctantly guided away by her mother's firm hand.

Finley took a seat next to Sebastien, and she took in anew how badly he'd been damaged.

'Is there a part that doesn't hurt?' she asked.

'It just looks worse than it is,' he said.

She wiped away a tear. 'Really?'

'No,' he said, then laughed, only to wince. 'Ow, I have a few cracked ribs too,' he added.

'Oh Sebastien. I wish there was something I could do. Can I get you anything? Water?'

He shook his head. 'No, I have all I want,' he said, reaching for her hand.

She smiled. 'Me too.' She closed her eyes, and couldn't help the tears that fell. 'I thought I'd lost you.'

He tried to sit up. His eyes were full of emotion. 'I know, I'm sorry.'

She shook her head, then took a deep, courageous breath as she opened up her small clutch bag and fished out a clean, knotted handkerchief.

'So, it's not my grandmother's ring or anything. But it is pretty special to me. I know we said, if we did this, there would be dinner somewhere special. But well, that's not how it's ever worked for us. None of us planned for the other, and I'm—' Her voice broke. 'I'm really glad about that.'

'Finley?' said Sebastien, staring at the handkerchief in her lap, a puzzled expression on his face as she unknotted it and took out a gold band. His lips twitched into a crooked smile. 'Are you proposing – is this really how you want to do it?'

She smiled. 'Yes.'

EPILOGUE

Finley and Sebastien got married in June 1941, when her favourite old-fashioned roses were in bloom. A few months later their daughter, Joy, was born. A beautiful baby with her father's eyes, and her mother's smile.

Christopher walked her down the aisle and Tommy Slopes made the long journey from Cornwall for the day with Robert the border terrier.

The members of the Finley Players each performed a short poem for the occasion.

Sebastien got a job as a journalist for the BBC, and would later become a senior news producer in television.

He had burns on two-thirds of his body and on cold days his left hand wouldn't open or close. But to Finley he was still the most beautiful man she'd ever met.

Finley finally got her big break after the war, in a lead role as an ordinary housewife who keeps the home fires burning and everyone's spirits up. The director who booked her was none other than Nigel Fitzpatrick, and he praised the fact that she looked 'just like the girl next door'. Finley didn't point out that once, a long time ago, he had made it seem like this was a bad thing. She did however tell him where he could stick it when he suggested she lose ten pounds.

The Finley Players would remain friends for the rest of their lives and, when Sebastien and Finley had a son in 1946, they named him after Archie.

Christopher became a lawyer, and got married to a French woman at the end of the war. They never had children but they did have four border terriers; they were all called Robert.

Isabelle moved to Cornwall and she and Marta were life-long friends. Isabelle set up a new haberdashery shop in the high street and Marta was hired as a hairdresser at the salon, where she developed a reputation for giving incredibly stylish haircuts but also insisting on knowing what would actually suit someone and not being afraid to tell her clients this – they loved her for it.

Katrin decided to follow in Finley's footsteps, and trained as an actress.

When the war was over, they discovered that Gunther had died of tuberculosis in the Dachau labour camp in 1942. The news was devastating, and they would spend the rest of their lives, like millions of others, trying to understand this bleak period in time, and to make sense of something that they couldn't. All they could do was put one foot in front of the other, and to take comfort that even in the darkest hours of humanity, there are always those who provide light amid the shadows.

A LETTER FROM LILY

Thank you so much for reading *The Only Light in London* and I really hope you enjoyed it. If you did, and want to keep up to date with all my latest releases, just sign up at the following link. Your email address will never be shared and you can unsubscribe at any time.

www.bookouture.com/lily-graham

If you did enjoy *The Only Light in London*, I would be very grateful if you could write a review. It really makes such a difference helping new readers to discover my books. Also, if you'd like to get in touch or find out more about my other books, you can do so through my website or social media.

www.lilygraham.net

facebook.com/LilyRoseGrahamAuthor

instagram.com/lilygrahamauthor

ACKNOWLEDGEMENTS

Every book is its own challenge and this one wouldn't have got here if it wasn't for my incredibly kind and patient editor, Lydia Vassar-Smith. Thank you so much for your wisdom, support and kindness.

My deepest thanks to the Bookouture team for their hard work and support, for the gorgeous covers, and everything you do.

My gratitude to the diary of Vere Hodgson, who really gave me a sense of wartime London, and provided the inspiration for Finley's job, in *Few Eggs and No Oranges: The Diaries of Vere Hodgson 1940–45*. Similarly, Margaret Kennedy's *Where Stands A Wingèd Sentry* offered a real insight into the months before the Blitz began and how ordinary people were truly feeling. Margaret's book in particular painted that sense of fear and the moment when it became clear that this would be a hard war.

Huge thanks to my family, near and far, for all your support and encouragement. My husband Rui, who always believes that the words will come, and to my little furry companion, Frankie, for being with me through all the late nights and early mornings, you always know just how to lend a paw and are my own little light source in dark times.

Last and definitely not least, thank you to you – the reader; thank you so much for picking up this book, and to all the readers and bloggers who have reached out to me and been so kind and supportive; it means the world.

PUBLISHING TEAM

Turning a manuscript into a book requires the efforts of many people. The publishing team at Bookouture would like to acknowledge everyone who contributed to this publication.

Audio
Alba Proko
Sinead O'Connor
Melissa Tran

Commercial
Lauren Morrissette
Jil Thielen
Imogen Allport

Cover design
Emma Graves

Data and analysis
Mark Alder
Mohamed Bussuri

Editorial
Lydia Vassar-Smith
Lizzie Brien